sloth

Mark Goldblatt

GREENPOINT PRESS
NEW YORK, NY

ISBN 978-0-9832370-8-2

Library of Congress Cataloging-in-Publication Data

· Second Greenpoint Press Edition, January 2013
· First Greenpoint Press Edition, May 2010

This edition designed by Robert L. Lascaro, LascaroDesign.com
Book text set in Minion Pro, text drop caps and cover title set in Buteco

Greenpoint Press,
a division of New York Writers Resources
greenpointpress.org
PO Box 2062
Lenox Hill Station
New York, N Y 10021

New York Writers Resources:
· newyorkwritersresources.com
· newyorkwritersworkshop.com
· greenpointpress.org
· ducts.org

Printed in the United States
on acid-free paper

Praise for Mark Goldblatt's SLOTH:

Dostoevsky permeates *Sloth*, especially *Notes from the Underground*, with its duality and layers of unreliable realities. Add a large lump of adoration for a TV aerobics instructor named Holly Servant, worshipped and wooed from afar by the love-struck diarist of this story, and you have what amounts to a word-rich ride, rollickingly inventive. . . . Goldblatt, the real one, the author self-reflexively observing the fictional one, could easily (if he wanted to) write literary pornography that would rival (possibly surpass) anything Robert Cleland wrote when he was obsessed with Fanny's fanny. But though *Sloth* doesn't shy away from things sexual, titillating sex is not its primary purpose, which is rather a philosophical search for identity. *Sloth* is a work filled with artistic flavor and Rabelaisian slumming. It is funny, serious, insightful and as unique in style and substance as any seriocomic novel I've read since Steven Gillis penned *The Consequence of Skating* or Junot Díaz wrote *The Brief Wondrous Life of Oscar Wao*. Some novels leave you with a smile. Some leave you thoroughly satisfied. *Sloth* does both.

— Duff Brenna, *Contemporary World Literature.*

Mark Goldblatt (the real one) has written a parody of postmodern novels in which he out-deconstructs the deconstructors. Layers of meaning and misdirection are everywhere (as well as a lot of word play and fairly low humor). *Sloth* is a wickedly funny, challenging and brilliantly written novel by an author of rare wit and creativity. Great fun for sophisticated readers.

— Lars Walker, *The American Culture*

"It's like a walk through a hall of mirrors strewn with banana peels. If Nabokov had played the Borscht Belt, he might have written *Sloth*."

— Charles Salzberg, author of *Swann's Last Song.*

"Mark Goldblatt (or so he calls himself) has gifted us with a literary rollercoaster that feels akin to Henry Miller navigating through an Escher lithograph. Characters merge in and out of each other, constantly imploding and creating new Bizarro World realities. Or do they? "

— Mark Goldblatt, Editor, *Starship Troopers, Showgirls, True Lies.*

"For a novel called *Sloth,* Mark Goldblatt's hilarious satire moves more quickly—and easily—than the wine at an English Department party."

— Nick Gillespie, editor, *Reason.com.*

"Can love survive the deconstruction of the subject? Can intention outlast the endless deferral of meaning? *Sloth* threatens to make my bookshelf collapse as all the postmodern texts scramble for safety."

— Patti White, author of *Tackle Box* and *Yellow Jackets.*

"Read *Sloth,* and like curvaceous movies such as Memento and Inception, you'll want to start over and read it through again to see what you missed. It's like a Rubik's cube that no matter how many ways it's turned, the colors don't quite add up. Nor would you want them to."

— Richard Holinger, *PIF Magazine*

"Mark Goldblatt is one of America's most uncompromising literary iconoclasts."

— John Podhoretz, editor, *Commentary.*

ACKNOWLEDGEMENTS

From the previous millennium: Mitchell Levenberg, John LiCastro, Stephanie Medina, Sal Salamone, Bob Wyatt, Sandra Schor and Robert Towers.

From the current millennium: Jonathan Kravetz, Linda Helble, Vivian Conan, Bob Lascaro, Sharon Gurwitz, Susan Altman and Scott Gould.

*I dedicate this book,
now and forever, to Holly.*

FOREWORD

From the PIF Magazine *interview*
with Mark Goldblatt by Derek Alger

ON A NOVEL CALLED SLOTH . . .

Derek Alger: You received a warm reception at a recent reading at KGB Bar in New York City's East Village.

Mark Goldblatt: That was part of the Trumpet Reading Series run by Jonathan Kravetz and sponsored by the New York Writers Workshop. I thought the evening went pretty well. It's always difficult to gauge the audience's reaction from behind the podium, but people seemed to laugh at the right places, and no one threw produce. I've read there before. It's a good atmosphere. Lots of writers in the crowd. Photos of Soviet villains on the walls. Occasional police sirens from the street below. It feels like the kind of place you could hatch a decent conspiracy.

DA: Do you do many public readings?

MG: I've been doing more readings lately in support of Sloth. That's part of the deal when you're working with a small literary publisher. You need to help generate publicity—since there's no ad campaign behind you, and newspaper reviews are few and far between. The upside, of course, is that you get individual attention, and you have greater editorial control. As for readings in general, I'm not a natural performer; if the material isn't up to par, I have the potential to bomb in a big way. But the book is funny, or at least it's meant to be funny, and it's full of word play, and that sort of thing tends to work when read aloud. What's Chuckles the Clown's motto? *A little song, a little dance, a little seltzer down your pants.*

DA: Tell us a bit about Sloth.

MG: The novel consists of journal entries written by a guy who gets paid to wait in long lines — literally, a waiter — who falls in love with a TV exercise girl. He tries to woo her by writing love letters, which means that the letters not only have to win her heart but also demonstrate that he's not a stalker. *Have you ever tried to convince someone you weren't crazy?* That's the first line of the book, the predicament. Eventually, she does write back . . . and asks the natural questions like: Who are you? What do you do for a living? The narrator realizes he can't tell her the truth — that he's a waiter — so he assumes the identity of his best friend, Zezel, a former newspaper columnist, who wrote under the pen name "Mark Goldblatt." Unfortunately, Zezel gets wind of what's going on, breaks into the narrator's house, and then into his computer and begins writing his own entries in the narrator's journal. Zezel's entries are risqué (which strikes me as a much nicer term than "pornographic") and mock the narrator's original love quest.

DA: The book's cover claims Sloth is a satire of postmodernism, while also being a postmodern satire, in which nothing is what it seems.

MG: Well, you've got the narrator (who goes unnamed) pretending to be "Mark Goldblatt" in order to woo the TV exercise girl, and you've got the narrator's best friend Zezel also pretending to be "Mark Goldblatt" — that is, when he's not breaking into the narrator's journal and pretending to be the narrator. Then, of course, you've got Mark Goldblatt pretending to be both of them in the act of writing the book. What I was attempting to do was poke fun at highbrow lit-crit concepts like the de-centered self, the fluidity of identity, and the death of the author — but to do it in a no-joke-is-too-cheap way. I wanted to write a book that would be slapstick page by page but would carry a darker subtext: the corrosive effect of postmodern cynicism on the human heart. The whole would make sense if you were a Norton anthology geek, if you had an ongoing affection for Dostoevsky, Dickens, Sophocles, Dante, Yeats, Nabokov, Philip Roth, Nathaniel West, Hamlet and The Merchant of Venice . . . as well as Aquinas, Descartes, Martin Buber, Henny Youngman, Mr. Ed and Dr. Seuss. Otherwise, it would just seem like an odd but (I hoped) funny book.

DA: But in what sense is Sloth a postmodern satire?

MG: In the sense that the form and the content are at odds. The outcome of postmodern literary theory is to level all literature, to render absurd the ranking of one text above another text. So I wanted to write a postmodern text that was, at its core, a celebration of dead white males or, in the case of Mr. Ed, dead white horses.

DA: You were fortunate to find a dedicated literary agent who believed in your work.

MG: Scott Gould is my hero. I queried him out of the blue back in 2004 and sent him the manuscript for Sloth. I didn't have high hopes; I liked the book and was proud of it, but I realized I'd written a quirky novel whose target audience was pretty narrow — really, literature professors, graduate students and other writers. Despite that, Scott took it on; he had a particular editor at a major house in mind and sent it out on an exclusive submission. The editor read the book and wanted to acquire it but was voted down by his colleagues. The easiest thing for Scott to do at that point would've been to cut bait. But he believed in the book and stuck with it. For the next five years, he blanketed the market; he was relentless; even after he switched agencies, he retained me as his client. Several more editors expressed interest but were voted down. Frankly, I was willing to throw in the towel. But every month or so, I'd get an email from Scott saying something like, "Hey, I was just talking to a new editor at Farrar, and I told her about Sloth, and she said she'd take a look, so keep your fingers crossed." Remember, the book hadn't earned a penny for him, and he'd been championing it for half a decade. We lucked out when Greenpoint Press, which had been publishing memoirs exclusively, expanded its mission to include fiction. Scott sent Sloth to Greenpoint, and the rest is history . . . obscure history, but history nonetheless.

DA: I can't help noting that you once lived on the same block as the Empire State Building.

MG: Just me and the Big Gorilla. I'm smarter, but he's way smoother with the ladies.

"He holds enough of torture in his own *ubi* and needs not the misery of circumference to afflict him; and thus a distracted conscience here is a shadow or introduction unto hell hereafter."

— Thomas Browne, *Religio Medici*

JUNE 8, 2000:

Have you ever tried to convince someone you weren't crazy? By all means, do. Tomorrow morning. Choose a stranger, not an acquaintance. Certainly not a friend—who knows you for the maniac you are regardless. Now, go ahead, explain yourself: "Despite appearances, sir, I am not out of my mind. Quite the reverse, it is sanity itself which moves me to this exercise. Sanity itself which moves me to accost you, to clasp you on the shoulder as we stand here, to speak to you with a familiar voice unearned by familiarities." With every word, with every gesture, the stranger withdraws. His eyes roll back, full of disdain. Still you persist, gathering his hands into your hands. Now his eyes start to widen. He is afraid. He glances up and down. He fears the stiletto you are about to produce. But from where? No matter, for he has shaken loose. He backs away slowly. As he turns the corner, you hear the sound of his feet. He is running.

Now these are the most opportune of circumstances. Daylight. Eye-contact. The wry monotone of a sane man's voice to offset the act. What I propose is far more difficult. For I have fallen in love with an exercise girl named Holly Servant who appears every morning on the television. What I propose is to woo her. To woo her from afar at first, to woo her with the words love has written upon my heart. To woo her on crisp, clean acid-free paper—for e-mail is too ephemeral, too case-insensitive, to convey the substance of what I feel. *Abelard to Heloise@mortalcoil.org*? I think not! No, paper it is. I will woo her on the page, perchance to bed her by my words.

The air was khaki today on West Forty-Fourth Street. Perhaps the soot on the window had prismed the remnants of sunlight, or perhaps it was the neon-skewed dusk of Times Square at an angle I had not observed before. No matter, I opened the window and breathed khaki air. It smelled of engine fluid . . . of engine fluid and fresh pralines. Sticky poison. But it was air, so I inhaled deep gulps of it. Four stories down, I watched a man in overalls as he stared under the hood of his truck. Steam rose around his head, khaki-tinted steam. He wiped his forehead with a gray rag.

The praline cart stood fifteen yards to his left, on the southwest corner.

There was a cluster of taxis at the intersection of Broadway and Forty-Fourth. Their horns were silent. Rush hour had passed. Now was the hour of khaki air, the hour of sticky poison and silent cabs and twilight. Saxophone music came up the street; it was from the blind man who worked the southeast corner, across from the praline cart. He played the same songs on the same street corner every afternoon, four o'clock to eight o'clock, rain or shine; this was his final song, "Yesterday." As the saxophone sounded, a homeless woman in a Yankees cap suddenly began to sway back and forth and sing:
There's a dog in the house.
There's a dog in the house.
There's a dog in the house.
There's a dog in the house.
There's a dog in the house.
There's a dog in the house.
As I leaned further out the window, I felt a sudden drop of water on my head. The sky was cloudless, the khaki air darkening to black; I squinted at the last traces of sunlight across the Hudson River. Then another drop of water hit me. The drops of water took several seconds to worm their way through my hair to my scalp. Then I felt for them,

the drops of water, with my fingertips. They were gritty. They had fallen from the air conditioner one floor above my window. As soon as I glanced up, another drop of water hit me in the eye.

JUNE 10:

Think me not insincere, gentlemen: I *do* love Holly Servant. Though I am by no means a sincere man, nevertheless, I am of a second spirit where Holly is concerned. The visible beauty of the flesh, it was once believed, testified to higher virtues of the soul. The inside was reflected on the outside since God made the world not to deceive man but to sustain him. And oh what virtues I discern in Holly Servant! Cut to close-up: There are angels aglow in her eyes, cool blue seraphim who whisk from side to side as she calls out the cadences. "C'mon," she urges, "just ten more, nine more, eight more, now seven . . . " From the bare floor of my studio apartment, I find within me the final ten. The muscles of my stomach feel like hot wires, and sweat trickles into my eyes, but still I find her ten more. As much as by her eyes, I am driven by the sing-song of her voice, the lilt even as she launches into twelve minutes of aerobics. Now, though, I only watch—for the sake of the downstairs neighbors. Yet also for my own sake, for I watch the dizzying metronomic dance of her areolae, shining like tulips through her leotard. By the end of the segment, she has sweated her various definitions into the cotton. Then, at last, the cool-down. She rolls her head from side to side, strands of her pixied blond hair clinging to her moist back and shoulders. She stresses the cool-down especially. "Make sure to give yourself at least fifteen minutes for your heart rate to come down—and *never* exercise to the point of pain or exhaustion." Common sense, to be sure, but she takes the time to caution us, to belabor the safety factor. Because she cares. The emphasis on the word "never" is desperate—as if she'd never be able to forgive herself if even one viewer overdid it. Then at last she signs off, and always with a piece of wisdom or a metaphor: "Life is like a card game, and the Sunrise Workout is like your ace in the hole. Play it, and rake in the chips for the rest of your life."

Dear Miss Servant,

And you are dear to me, Miss Servant. That sounds
presumptuous, I am aware. Nor is it my custom
to address letters to people I have not met. But I
have broken with custom, perhaps with decorum,
in this case—because certain instances arise in
life which beg, which even demand, words. So I
write to you, for I cannot speak them. Fate has
determined us strangers, and I would not broach
Fate beyond these several lines. Nevertheless, you
have grown dear to me. Yours is the first face I see
every sunrise, the first voice I hear every morning.
Let me tell you about my alarm clock. It is a shrill
thing, a loud electric buzz, set on a stand beside
my bed. As I sleep, the clock rests less than a
foot from my ear. When it goes off, it annihilates
whatever dreams are left inside me—I am not
awakened so much as galvanized. That was before,
of course. Now I welcome the sound, welcome the
annihilation of my dreams. For the sound has come
to signal your dear image on my television, your
kind words within my room. When you speak to me
of life, I am filled with hope. For myself, of course.
But also for the world. Life is good, Miss Servant.
Though babies starve in the Third World, though
holocaust hangs upon the air, though disease and
violence race through the streets of our major
metropolitan areas, despair has no place in the
heart of man. Let him only look to the Sunrise for
his inspiration.

Sincerely yours, etc.

Hours have passed; I am no longer certain of the time. The letter
is posted. But how the images linger! How the images move me, how
they move my fingertips across the keyboard! Oh, let me celebrate love
in the name of Holly Servant: She who would have me touch my toes

twenty-five times per day, in her name I touch many things besides. Was there a life before Holly? Naturally, yet it was something less than life. Those were dim disembodied days, up perhaps at the crack of noon—*to wait*. For that is, in fact, the livelihood I have chosen, the livelihood I have invented.

I am a waiter.

That is to say, again, I *wait*. It began one morning at the Department of Motor Vehicles. (What better place for an autodidact?) I stood on a line that bent twice before it angled into a single arc that circumscribed the entire second floor of the building. My nose was buried in Kafka when I happened to overhear a conversation between two suits in front of me; they were commiserating, in deep cynical voices, over the sums of money each would lose in the hours until their turns came up. Finally, I took pity on them. I suggested, without a thought of profit, that if one of them would lend me his mobile phone, I would be glad to call them when the wait had wound down to fifteen minutes.

They eyed me with suspicion at first. But then, perhaps sighting Kafka, shrugged at one other, and the taller one unholstered his black telephone. When at last I summoned them, and when at last their turns came up, I received a tip of one hundred dollars. Plus, they wrote down my name in one of their black binders—a gesture I have always found complimentary. Within a week I was receiving two or three requests per day. I became a familiar face not only at Motor Vehicles but also at several downtown post-offices, outside theater openings and movie premieres, at Knick and Ranger Ticketron outlets, etc. Nor was I highfalutin: I would sit in cars until alternate side of the street parking regulations went out of effect or in limousines as their drivers stepped out for fellatio. Always, of course, I scaled my fees in accordance with the client's ability to pay.

No, nothing *is* served by such particulars, I concede. Especially since the letter to Holly Servant is posted. The sun burned against my forehead as I slid the mailbox shut. For an instant, I stared into the sun. Then I closed my eyes, and the sun was inside my head.

JUNE 21:

Still no answer, but I find no reason for concern. There are, to be sure, channels that correspondence with celebrities must follow—secretaries, agents, bomb squads and the like. I have no illusion that Holly Servant's eyes will be the first inside the envelope. Meanwhile, life goes on. Yesterday, her message cut to the very core of the modern *ennui*: "No one likes to exercise," she declared. "But everyone likes to look good. If we exercise, we look good. It's as simple as that." How true! How true! Ours is a tradeoff existence, a bargain basement of spiritual beads and trinkets for which we pay blood—this, in anticipation of a greater reward on the higher floors. But what if there are no higher floors? What if the escalators lead nowhere?

Holly's point, indeed, was driven home in an unanticipated way last night. As I hurried past Full Pockets, the male strip-joint over on Eighth Avenue, I was accosted by a bruiséd kid. (I prefer the poetic "bruiséd," accented in a nineteenth century tubercular manner, to "gay," which is too optimistic, or "homosexual," which is too clinical.) And he was a *kid*, maybe seventeen or eighteen, and whether he was bruiséd by nature or by necessity I haven't a clue. But he grabbed me by the left arm and shot me a desperate bruiséd look. The only words he spoke were: "Want to party?" Now the first thing I thought was how fortunate he was to have chanced on me, since I wasn't going to lash out. From his looks, the same suggestion had cost him in the past. There was a blue-green half-moon, a perfect crescent, beneath his right eye, a cracked tooth in the front of his mouth, and a scar down the center of his chin. And there was a plea in his voice, a moist desperation in the three words he spoke, a plea too in the way he clung to my right arm. . . .

Yet I declined; I shook loose without saying a word, wrested my left forearm from his grasp and hurried the rest of the way home.

Decorum, gentlemen! Decorum, at all cost!

JUNE 27:

Critical questions are the cross I bear. This is perhaps the effect of too much time on my hands, or perhaps too much starch in my diet. Zezel lectures me about my diet on a regular basis.

Zezel is not his actual name; I withhold his actual name in case this journal should fall into the wrong hands. But I will allow this: Zezel is a friend of mine, perhaps a dear friend. Perhaps the dearest friend I've ever had. Perhaps he is my lover. Except you already know I am not bruiséd. No, Zezel is not my lover—even though there is much to love about him. Think of Zezel as short. Think of him as thick, short and thick. Think of him under wisps and curls of thinning blond hair. No, Zezel and I are not lovers. Nevertheless, he is concerned with what I eat. As we sat in the corner booth of the Kosher Deli last week, he shook his index finger and cautioned me against a side order of potato pancakes. "Too greasy," he said.

"The world is too greasy," I said.

"Which world? What is your reference?"

"*This* world."

"The one the Jews control?"

"No, not the media . . . I mean, the very quiddity in which we find ourselves."

"So it is written," Zezel said.

"So it shall be done."

"Spare me your speech acts." Zezel smiled, then narrowed his eyes in a mischievous way. "Do I smell a nominalist?"

"I stink: therefore, I am," I said. "Good shtick?"

"Good shtick," he said.

Then we started to eat.

Zezel is an odd case. He is my dearest friend, yes, but an odd case. Once upon a time, when we were young and able-bodied, the two of us planned to become writers. Men of our words. But who would have believed us? Even after I lost faith, however, he persevered. For several years, he wrote unsigned obituaries for a local paper; then he graduated to unsigned fillers, then to unsigned news, and he wound up, before he turned thirty, writing a weekly human interest column for a well known New York tabloid under the alias "Mark Goldblatt." (He refused to explain the significance of the name, if any. Probably, the sound of it amused him.) His columns were, on the whole, unremarkable—folksy, sentimental pieces as far removed from Zezel's true self as the byline from his true name. Regardless, he kept to his schedule of a column every seven days for exactly fifty-two weeks.

Then it happened.

Where once he had been prolific, prodigious, knocking off unpublishable novels and mock epic poems between columns, now his output slowed and then ground to a halt. He began to miss deadlines. The first week, the paper reprinted an old column. The second week, they withheld his check. Still, he could not write. He was blocked. He telephoned to tell me. "Why not just write?" I asked. "Whatever comes, comes."

"It's not that simple," he explained.

He was right, of course, it wasn't. He was blocked and then some. He was dammed. Not a trickle got through, not a sentence, not a word. He trembled even to sign his name. The paper canned him after he missed a seventh consecutive deadline.

Perhaps he ought to seek professional help, I suggested.

He stabbed me in the left hand with a salad fork. He stabbed me without a word, then lunged at me again, across the table at the Kosher Deli, and I took three stitches between the third and fourth knuckles. It was an awkward moment in our friendship.

Afterwards, in the emergency room, he wept, and then at last I realized he would never write another column. He used his resume of publications to secure a university line, and he has since recovered to the point that he can scrawl brief comments on the backs of his students' essays. But he no longer thinks of himself as a writer and will not acknowledge conversational references to his work. He has renounced that part of his life and all of his acquaintances from that period.

Except me.

JUNE 30:

Nothing on the desk except the cable and telephone bills. Nothing on my mind except time. Nothing in the mail this morning. What I am wondering is this: If it were possible to surrender up the next dozen hours, if it were possible to will tomorrow on the world twelve hours ahead of schedule, if it were possible to command the Sunrise, would I dare? Consider the consequences. Perhaps it is a Wednesday, and I have awakened with the certain knowledge that nothing is going to happen. The thing to do, then, is to will the onset of Thursday. But that's the danger, isn't it? For once I had begun, sooner or later I would surely will myself to death.

But never mind: I am, for the moment, a man of expectations.

JULY 6:

> Dear Loyal Viewer:
>
> Thank you very much for your kind words and your continued support. By the way, are you aware that the Sunrise Workout is now available on video? Bess, Holly, Nicole and the rest of the girls have personally selected their favorite routines from among the hundreds you have seen them perform. Each two-hour cassette is available at your local video outlet, or you can make your purchase directly from Sunrise Productions by visiting our website at *www.sunriseworkout.com*. The special discount price is $19.95, plus postage and handling. Please be sure to specify which tape(s) you want. Sorry, no C.O.D.
>
> -Sunrise Productions
>
> P.S. The girls do not have the time to answer all of their correspondence individually. Rest assured, however, that your letter has been forwarded to the person to whom it was addressed.

JULY 7:

> Dear Miss Servant:
>
> Thank you for your response to my letter. Rest assured that if I owned a VCR, Sunrise cassettes would be high

on my shopping list. This is true even though I am not, by nature, a list-keeper; I am more of a play-it-as-it-lays type, the type whose priorities fall haphazardly within the sweep second hand of his peripheral vision.

This has always struck me as a character flaw, actually, the kind of thing for which there should be a French expression but isn't. It is the peculiar gift of the French, I have noticed, to encapsulate what is not there, to conjure up ideas out of the lack of ideas, to wrench the seething *quoi* out of the *je ne sais*.

It would take a Frenchman, Miss Servant, to grasp the grasping quality of this exercise — for my writing to you is, in its own way, an exercise. Surely, you must appreciate that. I am toning my soul by the sincerity of these words as certainly as I am toning my flesh by the sound of your voice. I am stretching and twisting to reach you, driving beyond the limits that life has set for me, driving beyond myself. Not literally; I would not be so bold. But I am reaching towards the idea of you, towards the better man I am when I am involved in that idea. Your face hovers before me as I write. These moments, therefore, are redeemed.

I hope you will not be put off by that sentiment, Miss Servant. I know it is forward. But do not be alarmed. The fact that you have inspired me, body and spirit, is much to your credit; I am not easily inspired, and I thought it worth the effort to inform you. The effects we have on others are often, too often, unknown. In this case, at least, you know. Your moments in front of the camera have not passed in vain. You have made a difference in my life. That is the sum of what I intend to say.

Sincerely yours, etc.

No, gentlemen, I am not discouraged by her response. Though

she had no hand in the form letter, there is no reason to doubt that she has, in fact, read those first lines of mine—or that she will, in fact, read these new lines. What is critical to recall is that Holly Servant fills the air, wafts from antenna to antenna, from coast to coast, tightens and tones the warp and woof of her flesh to the pulse of a million picture tubes. We are a state-of-the-art culture, and these are high-tech times. My love has been pre-recorded and disseminated, freeze-framed in mid-extension to salve the despair of a nation. How could she fail to elicit many passions? To think that I am the only one . . . well, where I come from we have a name for someone like that. Solipsist. But I am no solipsist. Nor is my imagination capable of Holly Servant. She is for me the link, the glue by which to bind the self to the world. She is what Descartes sought, what in retrospect he never found. She is: therefore, I am.

But this is rarefied stuff, mental calisthenics, conceived on the head of a pin. With what allegorical notions I embrace Holly Servant! Meanwhile, the world presses in on me. Zezel phoned not five minutes after I had received her letter, so of course I had no shtick for him. Perhaps I have offended him. He has been known to erupt, true, but also to bear offenses without a peep—and it is the latter which makes the thought that I might have offended him unbearable. Better a kick in the groin, or a fork to the hand. Last year, for example, a lover of mine slapped me so hard that she knocked out a dental crown. For that I blessed her. But once upon a time I left another lover curled up naked on her bed, her faint sobs sunken into the mattress. What welled up inside of me as I departed was terrible, almost unspeakable; it was like a hot towel wrung in my colon. The recollection itself wrings the towel again. The recollection of the slap does nothing.

Time to set aside the keyboard: I shall call Zezel.

Zezel has a proposition, and for the sake of our friendship I cannot refuse. His wife has found a woman for me—as though I were not in love! The affection I bear Zezel must see me through this ordeal, as it has before. When Mrs. Zezel was twelve years old, she won a pink ribbon for her arrangement of a doll's house. It was a statewide competition, back in whatever Midwestern state Mrs. Zezel is from. That is beside the point. But as she recounts her triumph, she can recall the precise details of each miniature room; she swears that she can reproduce the entire house, and I for one believe her. The trait has translated into her adulthood. Now Mrs. Zezel is a keen organizer, a social broker, a builder of metaphorical doll houses in which to settle her friends. She does not like me, I am not her friend, but I am Zezel's friend, so she is at work on a doll house for me. Whenever I protest, Zezel only shrugs.

Mrs. Zezel does not like me, but if I were married she would like me. If I were divorced she would like me, or if I were widowed. Then at least there would be a foundation, a collection of trenches dug deep into the spiritual landscape, on which to raise another doll house. If I were bruiséd she would like me, but she would not allow Zezel to play with me anymore. I am none of these however, and she knows it. "What is he?" she asks herself. Nothing comes to her. How can she build her doll houses unless she knows what goes on inside? She loses sleep over this, I am certain. She would be rid of me, but she would not break Zezel's heart. *What the hell*, she thinks, and starts in on the doll house regardless. Perhaps now she can get some sleep.

Mrs. Zezel does not like me for a number of reasons, to tell the truth. The fact that I am not married is only the symbol, the crowning touch, the last straw. Where do I begin? She is a woman of *therefores*, and I am a man who lives on the other hand. She is the type who would continue to signal turns if she were the lone driver left after a nuclear holocaust; I once lost a car in a parking lot and never found it. She is a Vassar Girl, finished long after finishing went out of fashion. So she talks tough, *summa cum* sassy. She is, in sum, the very locus of reason, a geometric proof of a soul, hemmed in by her own *hences*, and hence defenseless. I feel for her. This, she suspects, and she waits for me to slip up or perhaps even to come clean and confirm her suspicion; she wants a confrontation. Instead, she gets smiles. Nothing but kind smiles. Nothing more terrifying than that. Like all logical people, Mrs. Zezel is terrified. Terrified of the world, of the simmering randomness of the world, terrified it will bubble over into her lap. Terrified of herself. Terrified of being found out. So she plays it cocky, devil-may-care, a cross between Lauren Bacall and Leo Gorcey. She married Zezel fresh off her own nervous breakdown, even though the two of them are a physical mismatch, in order to embrace and, perchance, subdue her terror; she married Zezel because he is entropy incarnate, a lunatic throb of unfocused unusable energy. Fresh off her nervous breakdown, she married Zezel in order to define her own sanity by contrast. To that extent, she has succeeded. But Zezel will not be domesticated. She married Zezel to keep an eye on him, to study him. To find out what she was missing and smother it with love. She still hasn't a clue. If he were not married, she would not like Zezel either.

He married her because she was pretty.

She is on her way over to brief me. Zezel has warned me in the past not to—

"Look at this place," were her very first words. "You've got books scattered on the floor, clothes scattered on the furniture. It just isn't normal. What kind of woman is going to spend the night in a dump like this?" She eyed me for an answer, but I had none. "Look, kiddo, you're a babe and all that. No one's gonna say no. But looks only get a woman to your doorstep. What gets her inside, what keeps her past the first drink, is character. Got any liquor?"

"No," I said. "None."

"What about beer?"

"None whatsoever."

"Have you ever seduced a woman?"

"Define *woman*."

"Okay," she said. "I get the message."

"Would you like a Yoo-hoo?"

She waved her hand. "Okay, let's get down to cases: Her name is Allison Molho. She's thirty-two years old and quite a dish—"

"So are you," I said, which was the truth.

"Maybe when I was your age . . . " Mrs. Zezel glanced behind her, perhaps to hide a blush. She is seven years older than her husband, nine years older than I am, but the suggestion that those years have worn on her is false. She is sculpted of harder stuff. There is an aristocratic air about her features, which are angular and ageless. Zezel carries photos in his wallet; even as a child, she looked like an adult.

"Even now," I said. "Though I think I prefer your hair shorter. As a rule, I like short hair. Not too short, not collaborator-short, but not past the shoulders. Past the shoulders, it gets . . . I guess *redundant* would be the word."

"Tough titties, kiddo," she said. "Allison's hair goes straight down her back, right down to her hips."

"That's all right," I said. "No one's perfect."

"Lay off, for once," Mrs. Zezel said. "For your own sake, not for mine, because I've got a hunch about this, about you and Allison."

"What about you and your husband?"

"We're just peachy," she said, then wavered. "Unless you've heard different—"

"No, that's not what I meant," I said. "Will the two of you handle the arrangements, or am I supposed to phone this Allison person myself?"

"Whichever."

"Let me think about it," I said.

"Not too long—"

"By tonight, I promise."

Zezel phoned less than five minutes after his wife departed. He wanted to know whether I had forgiven him—bless his Zezel heart. He was against the blind date, he swore, and if I chose to back out now he would understand. What about his wife, I inquired. Never mind, he would make her understand. If she wouldn't understand, then he would divorce her. He swore to me he would divorce her if she would not understand. Even though he loved her, he would divorce her. "For your sake," he cried. "For your sake, I'll start the litigation tomorrow. Only, please, allow me one more night. That's the sum of what I ask, one more night. Nights are too long to spend alone. After the deed, especially. Nights were made to rethink. If she comes to me in the night, as she is wont to do, will I have the wherewithal to stand firm?

What I fear, especially, is our inertia. We are each of us settled into a side of the bed, a toilet schedule. She knows the things I like . . . the naughty things. She doesn't laugh at the noises I make. Better, I think, to start the litigation in the morning, so that by the following night the deed has gathered its own momentum."

"Good shtick," I said. "Tell her to make the arrangements."

JULY 10:

How life tugs at the soul! When I heard Holly's voice this morning, I would've dissolved into the air, mingled with the radiations that bring her to me. But I had to pee. It snuck up on me, and at last I had to desert her image in order to pee. The indignities of the flesh are to be suffered, I suppose, towards a greater end. Yet when the spirit is raised with every Sunrise, what is served by such baseness?

Questions without answers . . . these are the worst things in the world. Still, I'd ponder them *ad nauseum* rather than face Allison Molho across a candlelit supper. But wheels are in motion. Arrangements have been made for tonight. There was almost a reprieve, a last minute call from the governor. Zezel still had not yet recovered from his intestinal flu; I could hear his heaves in the background. "Ah, Bartleby," I sighed.

Ah, but Mrs. Zezel would have none of it. She informed me that she had already changed the reservation at the Tijuana Room. Dinner for two instead of four. She would attend to Zezel's digestive survival. She would leave Allison Molho to me. "Now don't give me a hard time, kiddo. Don't make me come over there and brain you."

That, I did not want.

As for Allison Molho, I've nothing against her. Save for the love I bear elsewhere, Zezel's description of her would have won me over. He was lascivious and graphic, diamonding his thumbs and forefingers below the waist to indicate what the fuss was all about. That was when he first took ill. The next afternoon I proctored an exam for him at the University, where he teaches introduction to literary jargon. I permitted his students to cheat, as per his instructions. Zezel believes, and not without reason, that his students learn more by their machinations to cheat than by honest preparation for an exam; they tend to keep crib sheets in greater detail than notebooks. He once found a comprehensive outline of semiotics inscribed on a single Kleenex. Perhaps it is the euphoria of the criminal act which drives students to such excesses. Perhaps it is desperation, pure and simple. Whatever the efficient cause, Zezel has learned to capitalize on the effect. For that, I admire him.

Where oh where has the afternoon gone? Soon, too soon, I'll have to put on clothes. Now here is a confession: I compose naked. To be naked with your own words is critical. Clothes are clichés, and the ongoing temptation is to wrap inspiration in clichéd precedents. As though the muse descended a logical staircase! As though her bare ass could be pantied! Byron, for one, understood this. In the end, he laid aside his abstract theories, took up causes, and set out to fuck Europe.

So I compose naked in order to minimize fiction. Not that I hold truth sacred. Quite the reverse: Lies constitute the greater percentage of what comes out of my mouth; it is perhaps my greatest accomplishment. To write the truth is onus enough. To speak the truth is barbaric, antisocial, downright mean. "Ah, Bartleby, but what *is* the truth?" Yes, I can hear Zezel doing Pilate even now; I can make out the skepticism in the slight crinkled upturn at the edges of his mouth. "The truth," he would say, "is no more than a wink, a conspiratorial wink, between the mind and the world."

I wink: therefore, I am.

Now then the time has come to clothe myself. The clothes make the man? Nonsense! The clothes *belie* the man. But what lies will I put on tonight? Stuffed inside a pair of jeans is the suggestion that I like to relax, which is as false as the spit-shine on my oxfords. The Tijuana Room, downtown, has no specific dress code, but it caters to youth and affluence. The affluence must be low-keyed, however, diluted with a twist of Marx as you pass below 14th Street. Inconspicuous consumption is the order of business, a conspiratorial wink between credit card and toll-free number. The Broadway riffraff doesn't get in, but why rub their noses in it? As for me, I am neither young nor affluent. Nor am I riffraff. As long as I keep my pants on.

Gentlemen: These details are not crucial. But to appreciate the audacity of my love for Holly Servant, you must take into account the utter baseness that I represent. (Still, I am naked before the keyboard.) Mrs. Zezel imagines me handsome, and I'll not quarrel with her. For I have seen photographs in which indeed I *appear* handsome. But in the mirror, I am diminished; I lose something. Perhaps it is the reversal of the image, or else the animation of doubt, but I cannot locate the handsomeness in the mirror. What I find are the incidentals: the thick brown hair, the high cheekbones, the broad and sunken brown eyes. The inventory comes to handsome. But in the mirror, the whole does not come together. Who knows why? As long as the world continues not to notice, in effect I am handsome.

The truth shall remain between us, gentlemen.

No, the time for truth is past. Now is the time to dress, or else the reservation will be at risk. Oh, for a VCR now! For a last glimpse of Holly, spandexed in pink, to see me through the ordeal ahead! She would disapprove of my trepidation of course; she would lower her faint blond eyebrows towards the camera and remind me to hurl myself into each moment, to disdain compromise, to take no prisoners. But I would counter that an evening with Allison Molho is in itself an insidious compromise. To hurl myself into such compromised moments would serve the anarchic impulse, nothing else. It is an impulse I must fight. The world is a china shop, and I am pure bull. The very fact that I am drawn to the crystal signals me to back off, to fade into the sunset with my tail between my legs. But what if a single piece catches my eye? Something about the shape, about the light it refracts towards the ground. Where are you, Holly? Flat on your back beneath the hot lights of the studio?

What are these moments to you?

JULY 13:

Mrs. Zezel is beside herself. She is furious that I failed to show up at the Tijuana Room. She phoned me this morning, after she'd spoken to Allison Molho, and called me a spoiled child, a prima donna without even the courage to walk on stage. When I attempted to compliment her on the metaphor, she hung up. Then she called back and said solemnly: "I feel sorry for you." She did not call me "kiddo"—which would have eased my conscience. If I were still "kiddo," then there would still be hope, the possibility of absolution. She might have said, "I feel sorry for you, kiddo," and, in the end, forgiven me out of exasperation. But I'd offended her beyond wisecrack, beyond persona, out of voice. The insults gushed from her in a rehearsed treble rage. I had no defense; I merely absorbed her words. "Not even the guts to call and cancel . . . " No, I hadn't phoned Allison Molho. But not for lack of guts. What I lacked was a lie: I walked the bare wood floor, naked, until midnight, and then I went to bed. Yet even as I crawled under the covers, I was bracing myself for Mrs. Zezel's wrath. The consequences of my act, or my non-act, were plain to me, and I accepted them. That is not cowardice. That is not gutless. The gutless man would have borne the date to escape the wrath.

As I was about to explain this to her, Mrs. Zezel hung up again.

Zezel was quick to disassociate himself from his wife's judgment as he treated me to lunch at the Kosher Deli. Against the clatter of dishes from the kitchen, he spoke with baritone remorse about the tension between Mrs. Zezel and me. "She's got a heart as big as a whale," he said; as he said this, he cupped both of his hands in from of him, as if to describe two breasts. But Mrs. Zezel is built more like a dancer, high at the chest and petite at the waist. It is Zezel's custom at difficult moments to retreat to our childhoods, to reaffirm the maleness at the base of our friendship. We used to shoot baskets, Zezel and I, and he would pantomime a girl's breasts after I allowed him to win. He would recount an imagined assignation the night before: "Ran her from baseline to baseline, swishing from every angle." Then he would fire the ball inside to me for a lay-up. As I intentionally clanged the ball off the iron, he would add, "Got to rise above the rim if you want to jam."

"The White Man's Burden," I said.

"Had a hand in my face the entire night," he said. "But I was on fire. I was in the zone."

"When you feel it, you feel it."

"But what of you? Still boxed out?"

"Can't even get on the court," I replied . . . even though it was an untruth, and both of us knew it. But it was important to reassure him. Zezel was a virgin when he married Mrs. Zezel.

As he cupped his hands before him now, he meant to remind me of those days. As though he had to! The waitress appeared at our table, and Zezel even allowed me to order potato pancakes. "My wife . . . " he said, almost under his breath, and allowed the words to trail off.

"Forget it," I said.

The potato pancakes did not sit well, and I became lethargic for the rest of the afternoon. Then I took a bath and fell asleep in the tub. As I soaked, I dreamt an odd dream. Zezel and I stood at the very foot of the Cross, and he kept nudging me to leave. But I would not leave; I was caught up in the event, in the milkiness of the moment. Out of the corner of his eye, Jesus noticed the two of us and was about to speak, but he said nothing. Then Zezel said, "C'mon, let's get out of here. He knows we don't belong." Again, however, I would not go with him. Finally, he gave my arm a hard yank, and we found ourselves back, once more, in the corner booth at the Kosher Deli.

"Why did you do that?" I asked.

"Nothing would have been proven."

"There were answers to be had!"

"Perhaps, but not *proof*," he said.

Then I awakened in the tub and climbed out. The skin of my fingertips was numb and wrinkled, and I felt the curved impression of the porcelain still against my back. Puddles of water collected between my feet as I dried myself. There was not a thought in my head, only the faint drip-drip-drip on the tiled floor.

JULY 16:

erendipity has once again taken me by the hand. As I stood, mournful, before a stack of Sunrise Workout videocassettes at my local video outlet, I was filled with a sudden resolve: I *would* purchase a VCR! It was the sight of Holly Servant that inspired me, the sight of her face, her "C'mon!" smile, replicated on each of a dozen cardboard packages; she stands center-frame, between Nicole and Bess, the three of them, pink musketeers, underneath a skintight plastic seal, and she beckons the consumer to put his money where his mouth is. It was there, in the exercise and self-help section of my local video outlet, as I clutched handfuls of Sunrise cassettes to my breast, that the resolution came to me.

But I am a waiter: I can wait no more than the market will bear. How, I wondered, would I come up with the extra cash *now?*

The answer was provided within that very hour. Provided, as I mentioned, through sheer serendipity, the serendipity of a hot humid afternoon, of a sudden desire to splash water on my neck, of the fact that I was passing in front of the University library at the moment the desire to splash water on my neck overcame me. So I ducked inside. There, posted on the wall next to the men's room, was the answer. It was a brief advertisement, the size of an office memo. Volunteers were needed. Volunteers for a scientific experiment. Volunteers for cash.

The advertisement ended: *Interested individuals apply upstairs, Room 21B4.*

The woman in Room 21B4 was herself a doctoral candidate. She had a gaunt look about her, all throat and forearms, the rest of her concealed under a light green laboratory smock. The smock was for effect however, an assurance of scientific control; Room 21B4 seemed otherwise a run-of-the-mill office, a single desk and file cabinet, a computer and telephone. The woman explained, in matter-of-fact tones, the nature of the experiment: I would be asked to take green pills, which might or might not contain a new psychotropic drug, and also to maintain a log of whatever changes I detected in my moods or behavior . . . and if I detected no changes, I did not even have to keep the log. The lone condition was that I return every two weeks for a finger prick. I would be paid a hundred dollars per pricking for the next six months.

"Sounds good to me," I said. "Where should I sign?"

First, however, she ran down a list of background factors that would disqualify me from the study. Did I have a history of mental illness? Did I take a prescribed drug on a regular basis, such as an allergy medication or heart pill? Did I use any sort of topical cream or ointment?

No, no, twelve-hundred times no. Where should I sign?

Then finally she smiled and handed me the waiver. No sooner had I set my John Hancocks beside her several X's than she took the papers back and handed me a thin plastic vial of thirty green pills, one month's supply. "Take one in the morning, the same time every day if possible."

"One pill," I said, "each Sunrise."

JULY 27:

Dear Loyal Viewer:

Thank you very much for your kind words and your continued support. By the way, are you aware that the Sunrise Workout is now available on video? Bess, Holly, Nicole and the rest of the girls have personally selected their favorite routines from among the hundreds you have seen them perform. Each two-hour cassette is available at your local video outlet, or you can make your purchase directly from Sunrise Productions by visiting our website at *www.sunriseworkout.com*. The special discount price is $19.95, plus postage and handling. Please be sure to specify which tape(s) you want. Sorry, no C.O.D.

–Sunrise Productions

P.S. The girls do not have the time to answer all of their correspondence individually. Rest assured, however, that your letter has been forwarded to the person to whom it was addressed.

JULY 30:

Dear Miss Servant:

It is with much regret that, once again, I confess
the want of a VCR in my household. I cannot,
therefore, in good conscience purchase the
Sunrise videocassette series at this time. (But I
am working on it!) Such details must be difficult
to keep in perspective, given the volume of your
correspondence; I respect that fact. Nevertheless,
I confess that the mode of your replies has begun
to trouble me. Not that I ever anticipated a point by
point answer to my letters. For of course I am no
one to you. (Do not mistake that for bitterness; it is
simply the truth.) No, I am troubled by the standard
form of your replies only because it points to the
possibility that you have not seen either of my
previous letters. This grieves me in a profound way,
as you may well imagine, since their purpose was
to articulate the gladness you have brought into my
life. Now I ask you, Miss Servant, what is the point of
articulation unless there is a receptive ear? (As an
artist yourself, you must appreciate the dread that
besets me!) What good is a canvas hung in the dark?
An aria sung on the edge of an abyss? As the artist
bares his soul, he braces against the fallout, against
high-voiced outrage, against yawns of indifference.
But he cannot brace against the void. He cannot
brace for silence.

Miss Servant, what I crave, above all else, is
acknowledgment. In whatever form you please.
Scorn me if you must. Even your contempt would
be welcome, and perhaps not unwarranted. But I
shall go further; since halting the form letter would
constitute a positive act on your part, I shall happily
accept that as proof that my words have indeed
made their way to you. Do you see? For us, silence

is not silence. For us, silence shall speak with more eloquence than words. Forgive me if I am caught up in the situation. But there seems now a hint of poetry in it, a poetic paradox, a poem where no poem would serve. By all means, stop the letter! Let your silence serve to acknowledge the poetic feelings that are welling up inside of me.

Sincerely yours, etc.

The thought *does* captivate me, gentlemen. That much, I concede. The thought that Holly and I are about to collaborate on a poetic gesture captivates me. How could it not? Where there is collaboration, must not synthesis follow? But what is synthesis save a rarefied form of intercourse? As I folded the letter, I envisioned her hands on the edges, her fingertips across the lines, her lips behind the words. But were the words sufficient? Had the words substance enough to move her, to bring her to act on them? No doubt, a phone call would suffice. Direct instructions from Holly Servant's mouth would, no doubt, halt another form letter. It was a question of potency therefore: Were my words potent enough to move her to the telephone?

The question captivates me.

AUGUST 4:

Let it never be said that I am not a man of science. More than two weeks have passed since the gaunt woman handed me the vial of green pills, more than two weeks of Sunrises, and I have yet to miss a single dose. Two weeks, however, are enough to persuade me that I am part of the control group. For I have had no reaction, no hallucinations, no sudden seizures, no paranoia beyond the usual . . . *ergo*: control.

I am in control.

The norm is what I am. How quaint! The rule that proves the exception. The barometer. The benchmark. The yardstick.

C'est moi.

Holly, alone, can save me.

AUGUST 8:

f I lean out the front window, perilously far out, I can almost but not quite see the precise location where I was accosted by the bruiséd kid. The incident comes to mind because the *Post* published an account this morning of a seventeen year old male hooker bludgeoned to death in an alley five blocks south and two avenues west of here, on Thirty-Ninth and Tenth. The photograph that accompanied the story was inconclusive, a pair of shredded jeans and worn out leather boots sprawled out beneath a police blanket. So now I glance out the window, once or twice each hour, in the hope that the bruiséd kid will turn up. Yet there is also a morbid allure, an eroticism almost, in the idea that he won't, a chill that races through me at the prospect that he's dead. For if he's dead, then I have brushed with death, have crossed before the glint of the scythe. Around noon, I traced the outline of a crescent in the soot of the window. Then, as I lifted the window, the air outside was the precise shade of gray as the glass. It smelled of exhaust, the air, and I savored it. The smell of human labor, of people at work, of civilization on the rise. The City swaddles me with its vast numbers like a nervous mother. The distant honks of taxis salt my blood. Each honk is an answer. There are no questions. The pink and blue neon flashes of midtown hotels issue through the gray windows whether or not I look. Safe moments, unnatural moments. The City hugs me to its breast, holds me close against the sudden incomprehensible violence of the natural world. The bruiséd kid? Or just a bruiséd stranger? Regardless, the death of *someone* has, this very afternoon, moved me to tears.

The window is a dangerous place, defenestration aside. It is a wordless place. Without words, I am dangerous. After an hour or so at the window, I was interrupted. Mrs. Zezel turned up at the front door without warning. The buzzer downstairs hadn't sounded. When she knocked, I thought it must be a neighbor, a survivor like me, a fellow dweller above the squalor. I cracked open the door but left the chain latched.

"How's my timing, kiddo?" she said. "Got a woman in there?"

"No," I answered. "But I'm not dressed."

"Want me to come back?"

"Wait here for a minute." I unlatched the door and left it just open. As I pulled on a pair of pants, I could hear her shuffling outside in the hallway. "All right," I called out to her. "Come in."

She stepped inside without a word, strolled from one side of the studio to the other, laid her hands lightly on several stacks of books and journals as I buttoned my shirt. Her glance lit on a dense purple book, fraying at the seams and weathered with age. She ran her fingertips across the edges, then blew off the dust. "*Anglicanism*"?

"The Church of England in the seventeenth century," I said. "Thomas Browne, Lancelot Andrewes, Hooker and Bacon. The usual suspects."

"Sounds peachy."

"Just a bunch of white guys trying to make sense of things. That's what white guys do, you know. Make sense of things. White guys like it when things make sense. Cause and effect. Nice and neat. Order is what white guys like."

"You don't have to tell me about white guys."

"White girls too," I said.

"What's that supposed to mean?"

She narrowed her eyes at me.

"Nothing whatsoever," I stated. "Just the Church of England. The Elizabethan Settlement. The *via media*, so to speak. Stuff to talk about in crowded elevators. It's not as though anyone takes it seriously. The doors close, the elevator goes up. If you're on, you're on. What could be more Calvinist than that?"

"Why are you telling me this?"

"Some people like clichés, but I've always leaned towards obscurity in elevators. It's more prudent, if you ask me, since there's nowhere to run."

"All right, I get the point," she said.

"Weather is too risky. People have opinions about the weather. But who has a stake in the Anglican Communion?"

"You've never forgiven me for being a gentile, have you?"

"Maybe a commodities broker," I said. "Someone who trades in futures, I mean. But what are the odds of running into a commodities broker in our circles—let alone our elevators."

"All right!" she shouted. "Can you plug it for a minute. That's all I'm asking, kiddo. Just a minute of your time."

"Ah," I said. "Have you come to apologize?"

"Why should I apologize?"

"No reason," I said. "It was just a thought."

"The trouble with us, kiddo, is that we're two of a kind," she said. "We're both a little pig-headed—"

"I wouldn't say that."

"Why must you contradict every word that comes out of my mouth?" she cried.

"Sorry," I said. "I guess you're right."

She softened for an instant, but then she heard the words again in her head.

"Oh, what's the use!"

"No, genuinely, I'm sorry."

"Kiddo, you haven't got a genuine bone in your body."

"Maybe not," I said. "But if I did, I *would* be genuinely sorry. That's hypothetical, but under the circumstances what else remains?"

She smiled at this.

"What about Allison Molho?" I interrupted her.

"I never meant to intrude, kiddo."

"That sounds almost like an apology."

Mrs. Zezel glared at me, then softened again. "Whatever gets you through the night."

AUGUST 10:

The chill of revelation hangs on the air, gentlemen. The chill of revelation amid the swelter of August! The police have been here, have stood with casually unconcealed weapons on the bare floor of my studio. How large they were! The two officers, a detective and a patrolman, arrived at the front door ten minutes ago and produced a photograph of the bruiséd kid. The thrill was indescribable as I lied to them, as I shook my head from side to side: No, I hadn't seen him before. Then I took the photo from the detective, a black man with a round likable black moon of a face, and I stared hard into the image for another several seconds. Then, once again, I shook my head. No, if I had seen a face like this one, I'd be certain to remember. Because I'm good with faces to begin with, I explained, and because this particular one was memorable. Notice the deep set of the eyes, the bruised cheekbones. This face, I could not ever forget. As I handed the photograph back, the patrolman thanked me for my cooperation. The detective then handed me his card: *Detective Lacuna*. He scribbled his direct line at the local precinct on the back of the card . . . just in case I remembered something else, he said. Then the two of them moved on to the next apartment.

The chill hangs fast on the air, even though the police have been gone for hours. But there is a fever in my fingertips. Thoughts to loose on the keyboard. But what thoughts? The bruiséd kid is dead. He is as dead as the deadest person who ever died. As dead as Lancelot Andrewes. Their lives hang like numerators above the common denominator of death. But what if death is zero? What if death turns out to be a simple void, that terrible zero of our most terrible nightmares? Then their lives, our lives, also come to zero. Chills on the air of time. Nothing to do but linger and then pass.

These words blood my brain.

The bruiséd kid's name was Aubrey Collins. According to the five o'clock news, he was nineteen years old and worked, on and off, at Full Pockets as a bus boy. Local television crews have descended on my neighborhood; for a half hour, I watched them out of the window of my apartment. Then I headed downstairs. From a safe distance, I observed one of the crews set up and begin to interview passersby. The reporter was a brunette woman dressed in a pinstripe suit and jogging shoes—a practical compromise, I thought. Amid the whirl of crowd noises and microphone feedback, she remained calm. She grasped each person by the shoulder, steadied each interview for the camera. The camera itself was operated by a fat man whose tee-shirt bore the name of a softball league. The evening was hot and humid, and the stains under his arms were the size of Frisbees. Between interviews, I sidled up to him with a diet soda and offered him a sip. He was hesitant. "You a faggot?"

So I looked down at my feet, then back up again. "Do I look like a faggot?"

"Maybe a little," he said.

"What if I am a faggot?"

"Then I feel sorry for you."

"Why?" I said.

"It's not right, you know?"

"Not *right* or not *natural*?"

"Same difference," he said.

"What was the question again?"

"Nah," he said. "You're no faggot."

He took the can of diet soda and began to sip from it.

"She's very pretty," I said, glancing towards the reporter.

"Believe me, we got better back at the studio. That's the only good thing about the job. I haul this dinosaur on my shoulder for six hours shifts, but at least I spend my nights with uptown pussy. Strictly hands off, you know, but a guy can always dream. Anyway, I wouldn't get my hopes too high if I were you."

"What if I wrote her a letter?"

"She gets hundreds of 'em," he answered. "Guys ask her to marry them. Take my advice: Go find yourself some whore and make believe. When you get down to the nitty-gritty, they're all pink on the inside."

Zezel phoned just after midnight because he could not fall asleep. His voice had a faint echo to it; he had pulled the phone into the bathroom. He spoke in hushed tones so as not to awaken his wife on the other side of the tiled wall. He told me he was sitting on the toilet. Then he asked me to guess what color pajamas he was wearing. But I knew this was a trick question. Zezel hadn't worn a pair of pajamas since puberty. Still, he'd accomplished his purpose. The image of him, stark naked, on the toilet, was fixed in my brain. Now I couldn't sleep either. "Welcome to the far side," he said. But then he hushed himself again. His wife was a light sleeper, and he had actually once roused her with the sound of a pin drop. It was an experiment. He had stashed a pin on the nightstand next to his side of their bed and remained awake for an hour. Then he pushed the pin onto the wood floor. She started from her sleep and switched on the nightlight. He only grinned to himself and pretended to be asleep. But the following morning he stepped on the pin.

Now he said to me, "Tell me a story."

"Two policemen turned up at my door—"

"Not that one, another one. Tell me a story about heaven. About quaint angels and harp music and fields of windswept lilies."

"What if there is no heaven?"

"Then make one up," he said.

"All right—"

"And with sex."

"Angel sex?" I said.

"Conceive immaculate."

"God turned up at my door—"

"Before or after the police?"

"After," I replied. "The policemen were here before noon. God didn't show up until much later, around four. He was in a hurry to make vespers, so he dispensed with the usual niceties and got right to the point. He'd come to reveal to me my special place in hell. That in and of itself is of no special interest. But as we strolled through hell, God and I, we chanced on a soul apart from the rest—apart from the multitudes there, many of whom were familiar, in that he bore his endless torment with a certain satisfaction. At least, that was how it seemed to me. When I asked God about this, he spake unto me saying: 'Among all the men who ever lived, only this man has ever loved wholly and purely. He loved a woman of his town, a prostitute, but because he was a poor man, he was unable even to afford her services. Yet as she lay dying, he prayed to me, a fierce and emphatic prayer, asking only to take her sins onto himself so that she might ascend to heaven. This, I granted him.'"

"And what became of the prostitute?" Zezel said.

"That's exactly what I asked," I replied. "And here is what God said: 'Lilac petals ease her every step, and honey coats the back of her throat, but she mourns him, day and night, mourns the lover she never knew in life, and so she will mourn him until the end of time.'"

AUGUST 14:

Dear Loyal Viewer:

Thank you very much for your kind words and your continued support. By the way, are you aware that the Sunrise Workout is now available on video? Bess, Holly, Nicole and the rest of the girls have personally selected their favorite routines from among the hundreds you have seen them perform. Each two-hour cassette is available at your local video outlet, or you can make your purchase directly from Sunrise Productions by visiting our website at *www.sunriseworkout.com*. The special discount price is $19.95, plus postage and handling. Please be sure to specify which tape(s) you want. Sorry, no C.O.D.

-Sunrise Productions

P.S. The girls do not have the time to answer all of their correspondence individually. Rest assured, however, that your letter has been forwarded to the person to whom it was addressed.

AUGUST 16:

Dear M_____,

Please don't be mad if another form letter gets to you before this. But PR gets all our mail before we do, and I have no control over them. Actually, I don't have much to do with Sunrise Productions anymore. The workouts are taped on a four month lag, so the last segment I did should air sometime in September.

Let me say, first of all, that I'm just so flattered by your letters. Your words are so touching, they make me sad almost. It's so special, I think, to write like that. To find just the right words for what's on your mind. Sometimes I write poems, but I always throw them out. What I want to say is inside me, but it never gets on the paper. Maybe it's like you said, silence is the highest form of eloquence. For me, at least, I think that's true. A lot of times I get in situations when the wrong word messes me up. Like at parties. Last week Mr. Finkleman (my agent) introduced me to a well known writer. So I started to talk about Charles Dickens, who is my absolute favorite writer in the whole world, and how *Great Expectations* is my absolute favorite book, and how I always read it with the sad ending, the way Dickens wanted it, where Pip and Estella don't wind up together, and then out of the corner of my eye I noticed Mr. Finkleman. He was waving his hands at me and shaking his head. He was trying to warn me to shut up! But it was too late. The damage was already done. When I turned back around the writer was gone. Did I mention that I'm also an actress? Later Mr. Finkleman explained to me that writers always look for fresh faces, kind of like blank slates. The reason writers like blank slates is to fill them up with their own ideas, so the ideas will come across to the audience. So as soon as I opened my big mouth, I started to fill up the slate. By the time Mr. Finkleman managed to get my attention, there wasn't any room left. No wonder the poor man walked away!

But why bother you with my problems? Especially since I pay my therapist for that. Thank you again for your letters. It makes me so happy to know that someone out there has been touched by my work.

Sincerely yours,
Holly Servant

The words on the paper have quit their meanings, and still I am caught up in the sounds of them, the subtle play of syllables across her lips. She perhaps spoke each word as she set it down. Many writers do. If so, then I have made her lips move. For what she has written, she has written because of me. Because of me and to me: I am the efficient and final cause of her words. Again and again I've read them. And at the bottom, her name! The sounds of her name, the syllables . . . they leave me breathless. Sighs of the heart. The hiss and suck of life. The reason I have a mouth, the efficient and final cause of these lips. But once more, once more —

AUGUST 19:

> Dear Miss Servant:
>
> Beyond words, I am touched by the kindness of your letter. Beyond the words of the present at least. Perhaps in another age, the Late Elizabethan let us say, I might have been able to summon the words. Language was less self-conscious then. How it gladdens me, Holly, that you read Dickens! Please forgive me the presumption of your first name, but to talk of classic literature on a last-name basis is to render it a specimen—as in the professional exchanges of academics. Let me assure you, art ceases to be art when it is laid open and dissected. As I stand before a canvas by Titian, his allegory of Sacred and Profane Love let us say, do not speak to me of the particulars of its creation, of the geometry of the figures. Only allow me to wonder, to stand in silent awe. Likewise, Shakespeare. Spare me the deconstructive turn, but whisper to me a sonnet as I drift off to sleep. The sonnets, especially, were made to be whispered, spoken in hushed voices across a pillow. There is nothing of the chisel in them: "Past cure I am, now reason is past care / And frantic-mad with evermore unrest." These are lilac petals; I would lay my head upon them.

Along these same lines, Holly—again, forgive
me!—I am delighted to hear that you write poetry.
What is crucial to remember, however, is that the
end is not the sole justification of the effort. The
poetic feelings are significant in themselves. The
fact that you are moved to write, to bare parts of
yourself before the prosaic world, shows sensitivity
and depth of character. That is yet another
presumption for which I beg your forgiveness. For
of course I do not know you; I am no one to you. Yet
I would be grateful to read one of your poems. Then
again I cannot guarantee a fair evaluation. For as
I read each line, I will hear your voice—and where
there is your voice, Beauty necessarily follows.

Let me only add, in conclusion, that the news of your
departure from the Sunrise Workout has caused
me much heartache. My consolation is in knowing
that your decision to leave must have been well-
considered and that your dramatic career cannot
but prosper from this moment forward. Still, in your
quest to become a blank slate, please do not lose
sight of what is written upon your soul even now. For
it is a poem of Shakespearean loveliness.

Sincerely yours, etc.

Rather than mail the letter, as I had the earlier ones, care of
Sunrise Productions, I took a chance on the return address from Holly
Servant's envelope: Finkleman Enterprises in Reseda, California.
I would, at minimum, avoid another form response.

Zezel banged on the door five minutes after I came back from
the post office. He was out of breath, his pupils dilated, and there was
agitation in his voice: "For your sins, I will intercede!"
"What have I done now?"

"What does it matter?" he said. "I have overheard murmurs among the Uncircumcised, so we two must take a vow. Now, place your hand under my thigh—"

"I prefer not to."

"But if I buy you dinner? Perhaps a night at the theater?"

I shook my head: "No."

"Would you, could you, in a box?"

"Not in the dark. Not with a fox."

He frowned. "Then you are not the fruit of my looms."

"But still the cream in your coffee?" I said, hopefully.

"That, yes."

"Then wherefore have I sinned?"

"Allison Molho—"

"The Original Sin?"

"The very *malum*."

"It was never my intention—"

"Nevertheless," he said, "a wound has been wrought, emotions left shattered in the aftermath. But fear not, gentle pilgrim. I have undertaken to set the world aright. For your transgressions, I *will* intercede."

"My savior!"

"In a word, amen," he continued. "By the noon, on the morrow, Allison Molho and I will weigh your soul in the balance. Simultaneously, we will address kosher sustenance at the usual place. These things I reveal to you in the name of Usual Crowd—that you may pass the hours in reverent prayer and worship."

He turned towards the door and began to fumble with the latch. Then he turned back to me and shrugged.

"Good shtick," I said. "But the exit needs work."

AUGUST 25:

After the first few times I noticed him, it crossed my mind that the man who is following me might be a figment of my imagination—an effect, even, of the psychotropic drug I may or may not be ingesting every morning. So I was tempted to skip a dose. But in the cause of science. . . . Regardless, it has become evident since then that the man who is following me is real. Perhaps, though, he means me no harm. He is a stranger, which is at least a minor consolation. If he were someone I knew . . . now *that* would be cause for concern. Since he is a stranger, however, I have no clue as to his motive, and indeed am solaced by the thought that he may have no motive whatsoever. He appeared, once again, below my window last night; he was leaning, at the angle of a private dick, against the lamppost across Forty-Fourth Street. He caught my eye as soon as I glanced outside. Here was a man, I thought, on another man's tail. Beneath the amber glow of the street light, his face remained shadowed. All I could make out was a pair of bushy eyebrows and a broad nose.

As he lit a cigarette, I drew the blinds.

Then, as I stepped outside for breakfast this morning, I noticed him again. Now he sat in a parked sedan, a brown Chevy, which pulled away from the curb seconds after I emerged from my front door. I quickly lost sight of him; I smiled. But then, as I bought a bagel from a street vendor on the corner of Sixth Avenue and Forty-Seventh, I saw the brown Chevy again. What consoled me now was the clumsiness of his pursuit, the absence of a doubt in my mind.

No, gentlemen, it was not paranoia: The tail he was on was mine.

As soon as I returned home, I phoned Zezel. There was no answer. Then I glanced out the window again, and the man was gone.

Now that he is gone, the time has come for reflection. Why would a man bother to tail me for twenty-four hours? Not that my life isn't a source of ongoing fascination—for me. But this sort of outside interest is difficult to fathom. Still, the thought that I am being followed, though unnerving, is also slightly flattering. For a man's footsteps are his own, distinct and inalienable, and as the man with the broad nose dogged mine he must have acquired a certain likeness of me, an intangible concept cleft from the muscular reality, a platonic shadow. How I wish he'd approached me! The background I could have provided would surely have redeemed his effort. He'd have come to see how every detour of the morning fit into the scheme as a whole, how the particulars justified the thesis. Even the plain bagel I ate, which must have seemed a non-sequitur of a snack, in fact served as a logical link, a considered response to the Tabasco-laden souvlaki I'd downed the afternoon before, a precursor to a three course kosher dinner with Zezel tonight. The balance is critical, reflective of an ideal of personal well-being. Whence the ideal, you ask? Holly Servant, of course! He who is after the justification of my existence must know of Holly Servant! She is the axis, the direct line from the rational soul to its fixity in the groin: I am utterly defined by the sweep of her gaze.

Remove her, and I might as well have had a pretzel.

AUGUST 26:

Broad Nose is back! Perhaps, then, he was never gone. . . . No, he *was* gone. (I must not lose sight of what I know.) He was gone last night, and now he is back. Back below my window. Back against the lamppost. Even now, even as I write. It was after Holly dismissed me, after our workout, that I again noticed him. For a moment, I only stood at the window and gazed into the vastness of the sky; I took in the morning sun and wiped beads of perspiration from my forehead. It is my ritual to gaze into the sunrise; Holly has wrought in me simple pleasures, the innocence of the newly risen sun against my face. But then I glanced down at the street and saw him. Sweat stung my eyes as I ducked back inside.

Why me?

That is the question I am left with even now.

Zezel turned up at the door less than a minute before noon. The buzzer sounded as I stood naked beside the window, my back pressed against the wall, about to sneak another glance at Broad Nose. "It is I," Zezel shouted through the door. I clutched at my chest, stilled the sudden throb of my heart. I glanced outside: Broad Nose had left the lamppost and was now half way up the block, leaning on a mailbox, reading a newspaper. As I approached the door, Zezel used his key and pushed it open. He startled when he saw me.

His line of sight drifted downwards. "Noah, I presume."

I grabbed a bathrobe and covered myself. "My Ham."

"But quite the Shem where it counts," he sighed.

"Short shtick," I said. "But I'm glad you're here."

He was smiling broadly, giddily. "This is big."

"Bigger than the man downstairs?"

Zezel squinted. "What man?"

"The man who's following me."

"What makes you think so?"

"*Ecce homo.*" By the left arm, I drew him towards the window. Then I dropped to my knees and crawled beneath the sill, to avoid being sighted, then rose again on the opposite side. Zezel only watched me and shrugged. Finally, I motioned him to glance out the window.

"With the newspaper?"

"The very one," I said.

"He might be waiting for a bus."

"For the past two days?"

"The bus might be stuck in traffic."

"He hasn't lit a cigarette."

"That *is* suspicious," Zezel nodded. He gave the situation a moment of thought. "He might be a detective. There was, as I recall, a homicide in the neighborhood two weeks ago."

"Then why is he following me?"

"You might be a suspect."

"But I barely knew the kid," I said. "We said hello when we passed on the street. If we ever had a conversation of more than a couple of sentences, I can't remember it."

"I had no idea!"

"Do you tell me everything?"

"Except the dross," he responded.

There was an awkward pause.

"What if I told you I was in love?"

"Theoreticals confuse me," I said.

"I am in love."

"Conveniently so?"

"Quite the contrary."

"How contrary?"

Zezel glanced out the window again. "Allison Molho."

"No!"

He nodded his head as a blush spread across his pale face. Then he smiled, for a weight had been lifted from him with the confession. Zezel suffers with his own thoughts. Since he no longer writes them down, he is forever in danger of forgetting. He is oppressed by the fear of forgetting; it hangs over his conversation like Damocles' sword, with the result that much of what he says is rehearsed and encoded. He needs to pronounce his ideas before he loses them. The sound of the words, even now, had crystallized his intentions. Now he smiled because he knew what he was going to do.

What Zezel was going to do he did not tell me. Nor did I ask. He would have told me had I asked, but I decided it was better not to know. That is true in most cases. The darkened mind is the most secure one, the least likely to get in over its head. Zezel *did* mention that he believed Allison Molho loved him in return—even though she had not spoken the words. Until the words were spoken, he added, there was no problem. Then he crossed his arms and allowed the thought to stand.

"So the effect of language, you might say, is to reify rather than to clarify."

He bristled at my response. "I come to you with the better part of my affections, I come to you with tenderized particulars, and what succor do I receive? Linguistic VapoRub? Fie and fie again!"

"Please, forgive me."

"Why should I?"

"For his sake," I said, and glanced out the window.

"Very well," Zezel replied. "But only for his sake."

When he left, I watched from the window as he passed within several feet of Broad Nose. Zezel paused for an instant, hands on his hips, as nonchalant as Zezel gets, and continued to stare up the block towards the corner. Then, an instant later, he shot a last look back at my window, a shrug of a look, and moved on.

Within half a minute, Zezel had disappeared around the corner.

Then, at once, I was seized with panic. I tore off the bathrobe and stalked naked through the apartment, gesturing at the window and walls. I'd gotten myself hemmed in. But why? For the first time, I contemplated calling the police. Broad Nose had been around long enough, I felt, to qualify as a dubious character. Still, I hesitated. What if the police sent over the two men who had questioned me about the bruiséd kid? The patrolman and the other, the black man, Detective Lacuna?

Hemmed in.

For several minutes, I continued to stalk naked through the apartment. But then I came to an abrupt halt. I stood in a corner, shoulders to both walls, and shivered; then I sank down to my knees.

Gentlemen, I confess it: I wept.

He's been gone for over an hour now. Since dinner time, approximately. The thought that Broad Nose might break for occasional meals is a consolation, further evidence of his material nature. He's not a phantom. Had he been a phantom, of course, Zezel wouldn't have noticed him. But Zezel is my dearest friend, and he might have humored me. Dinner, on the other hand, I trust implicitly.

Still, as I stood at the window, deafened by the growls of my stomach, I could not help but wonder if Broad Nose had ever been there in the first place. The lamppost betrayed no trace of him when, after another hour, I stepped outside to inspect it. Not a shred of his jacket, not the imprint of his weight. There was no odor of surveillance as I ran my hand up and down the cool metal surface. Without thinking, I kicked the base. It sounded like a church bell. Several passersby slowed and looked over their shoulders. Their gazes seemed, for a second, to penetrate me. But a second later, they wandered off.

I bought myself a Blimpie and hurried back upstairs.

AUGUST 27:

Through the night, I prayed that Broad Nose would still be gone in the morning. Then, for a time, I dreamed that he was back against the lamppost when I awakened; then I awakened, and he was still gone.

I stood at the window and sighed.

After breakfast, I showered and headed downstairs. I was due for my third finger prick. I had set aside the hundred dollars from the first two pricks; thus, as I strolled down Fifth Avenue towards the University, my steps were quickened by the knowledge that I would be able, at last, to pay cash for a videocassette recorder.

The gaunt woman in Room 21B4 smiled at me, a brief professional smile, when I entered. As I sat down across from her, she set out her instruments on the desk: a jab, a slide, a gauze pad and bandage, and a bottle of isopropyl alcohol. She typed more data into the keyboard to her left side.

Then she turned to me again. "Have you experienced effects?"

"None that I know of," I said.

"Depression?"

"No."

"Euphoria?"

"No."

"Paranoia?"

"Nothing beyond the usual."

"That was a joke, wasn't it?"

"Apparently not," I replied.

Finally, she snapped on a pair disposable gloves and laid hold of my wrist. The moment that she isolated my middle finger was rife with innuendoes, though it would have been highly unprofessional of her to acknowledge them. As she was about to jab me, I muttered: "A Gentle Knight was pricking on the plaine."

The next instant, I got the point.

Afterwards, as she applied the bandage to the tip of my finger, she glanced up at me and said, "*The Faerie Queene*."

"You peeked at my resume."

"Just before, you quoted *The Faerie Queene*. I used to be a lit major. Before I changed to bio-tech."

"Quite a conceptual leap."

She shook her head. "I just decided I wanted to make money when I graduated."

"Ah."

She released my finger. "What about you? Are you a TA?"

"What's a 'TA'?"

"Teaching assistant."

"I'm not that," I said.

"Adjunct faculty?"

"No, I'm a waiter."

"Lots of adjuncts are waiters."

"They also serve, therefore?"

"Do you always talk like this?"

"Do you mean cryptically?"

"Well, that's a kind word for it."

"I don't follow," I said.

"I mean, don't you ever give it a rest?"

I thought for a moment. "If I gave it a rest, there would be silence."

"Does that frighten you?"

"Nothing frightens me."

"I don't believe that. *Something* must frighten you."

"No, literally," I said. "*Nothing* frightens me. Nothingness. The *nihil* of our very worst nightmares. That's what frightens me. I can handle the occasional ghost or vampire. I scoff at succubae. But *nothing* . . . that's a horse of a different color."

The gaunt woman handed me a crisp one hundred dollar bill.

Moments later, as I left Room 21B4, I thought: *Nothing. Brrrr.*

Mere blood, gentleman! I have bartered mere blood for rapture. Even as I write, I possess the image of Holly Servant. I spent the afternoon shopping for a VCR, the evening connecting co-axial cable, and now, at last, the night is ours. Mine and Holly's. I own two full hours of her: Holly, in her signature pink. The warm-up. The stretch. The floor work. The aerobics. The cool down. But then, towards the end of the tape, comes a sudden fade. The lights dim, then start to strobe. New music, louder music, the pulse of bass notes. Then, the sudden squeal of an electric guitar. Holly saunters into frame from the camera's left. She is leopard-suited, bare at the midriff. She is dancing, *shimmying*. As the tape ends, a director's voice is calling "Cut!" and Holly is cracking up.

SEPTEMBER 1:

> Dear M_____,
>
> Sorry it's taken me so long to write, but things have been happening so fast around here. Too fast maybe. It's like it's out of control, my life, like it has nothing to do with me. But then it *is* my life, no one else's. That's what's so scary. You see, I'm the person who got everything going. Or at least I was part of it. Mr. Finkleman has helped me so much, and I must give him a lot of the credit. Can you keep a secret? Sometimes I like to pretend that I've just won an Oscar. So I put on a gown and high heels and stand on the coffee table. (I always put down coasters so I don't scratch the wood.) For the Oscar, I use an old spelling bee trophy I won in grammar school. (I used to make good grades.) (I can't believe I'm telling you this!) But I think all actresses like to make believe. Only in my dream I already know who I'm going to thank. I even know what order! So right at the end, I'm going to thank Mr. Finkleman. Sometimes I think he has more confidence in me than I do. Ever since we decided to leave Sunrise, he has taken personal control of my career. Last week, he arranged for me to test for a sit-com. The plot was kind of silly, about four career girls who share a house at the beach. (I was the ditsy one!) I didn't get the part, but I did get to meet David Faustino. He seemed very nice.
>
> Meanwhile, I've been doing stunt work to pay the rent. Let me tell you, the Sunrise Workout was a piece of cake compared to some of the things I have to do now. Like yesterday, I had to fall down a long flight of stairs. So after four takes, the director suddenly decided that he wanted me to crash through the banister instead

of rolling to the bottom. But I didn't mind. What really
teed me off was that I missed Carmen Electra by a
split second. She showed up to run lines while I was
getting padded, and then she left. All I saw was her
limo pulling away. That's show biz, I guess.

Thank you again for your letters. The girl that
Sunrise got to replace me is very nice. I met
her when we first tested for the show. She even
reminded me not to chew gum during the audition.
She should be on the air before too long, and I'm
sure you'll be pleased.

Sincerely yours,
Holly Servant

Here is the power of literature, gentlemen: Even as a strange man
once more haunts the shadows beneath my window, the words of the
woman I love have raised me beyond his trespass.

SEPTEMBER 2:

Dear Holly,

How much your last letter has meant to me I cannot
begin to explain. At the very instant when the world
seems about to spin free of its proper orbit, your
dear words have again drawn all things back to
their center. Perspective is what I mean, Holly. What
I can see from my window is a vast wilderness,
a vast desert bleached by compromise; against
such a landscape, it becomes difficult to sort out
substance from ephemera. Clouds wander by like
tufts of cotton, but a moth on the screen looms like
a pterodactyl. That's when points of reference are
most necessary. We cling for a moment to what is
known, what is at hand, what is at heart, in order to
gauge the relative worths of all else. Every distance

can thus be deciphered.

Does that make sense? For it is urgent that we make sense whenever possible. Not because I fear the nonsense of life, but between the two of us, sense is what I want. What I crave. To that end, I pore over your letters; to that end, I parse the grammar until I have solved every nuance and elision. That should not frighten you, Holly. To have your words taken seriously, to have them considered and solved is the highest compliment one person can pay another—because to solve a word takes time, and time is finite. So if I take the time to solve your words, recall that time is irretrievable. There's no restoration of the hours, no retake if in the end the words do not bear out the effort. In that case, there is only remorse.

But I feel no remorse, none, for the hours spent with your words.

What remorse I *do* feel is at the prospect that I shall soon be deprived of you, of your voice, every morning. The thought of Sunrise without you, to be truthful, fills me with despair. Even though I have every confidence in Mr. Finkleman (for the simple reason that you have confidence in him), I am quite appalled at the stunt work you are doing. Look in the mirror, Holly! Would Da Vinci have set up the Mona Lisa as a dartboard? Did Michelangelo sculpt bowling pins? No human being has the right to commit violence upon a work of art: It belongs to the entire race. To the mirror, Holly! Don't you see? Art! Sculpted perhaps by Nature, or perhaps by God himself. Mere genetics cannot account for the image.

Sincerely yours, etc.

SEPTEMBER 7:

He has been gone for three days now, and I am about to reconceive him in the past tense. That will be a relief. For it is only in the present that danger operates, not the past or the future. (That, even though danger lurks in the future, crouches behind each twisting conjugation of the road; yet danger cannot get at us until we arrive, whistling mindlessly, with the present in tow.) If only we could walk backwards! To live in the past is to live perfected, to sidestep the worst of our memories, to dwell on a re-presentation of each joy. Perhaps I'd remain forever before my television, fixed before her face, fixed amid her voice, fixed between her breaths. Fixed forever beneath a certain sunrise, the first instant I ever laid eyes on Holly Servant. So I shall! What I was then is what I am: Spent like a plow horse at the end of a vast field, slumped forward like a corpse on the end of my bed, no will to rise up, no courage to fall floor-ward, the complete works of Dostoyevsky, twelve volumes, lying conquered in a heap next to my pillows. For no reason, I pick up the remote control from the nightstand and switch on the TV. The background music of an infomercial for famine relief soothes me like a balm, cellos and violins, and for a full minute I lay motionless with my eyes shut. Then comes a man's voice, a somber bass infused with the urgency of saving children's lives, pleading for donations. I do not like the voice. I am distressed by the phrase "tax deductible contribution." But the remote has slid from my grasp, and I am too tired to reach for it on the floor. I have surrendered to the moment, to my inability to save the children.

But now another voice, the voice of an angel. Now her face comes into focus on the screen, and as the camera pulls back she sits cross-legged and speaks directly to me: "Get up!" she tells me. "Get up! Get up! Get up out of that bed, get up off that sofa, get up from that chair! Go ahead and go for it!" The effect of her words is electric. I am up in an instant, and in another instant I am down. She is down before me, and together we limber up on the floor. By the first commercial, I have broken a sweat. The czarist evils stream out of me. Breath comes hard. The half-hour routine she runs me through is merciless. I deserve no mercy. *Kill me!* I think. My heart is going to explode. But then the session ends, and her voice has lowered to a whisper. What she whispers is this: "Be good to yourself."

She smiles, and I am reborn.

Gentleman: I am suspected.

It was just after noon, a sun-dappled afternoon, and I was on my way out, on my way to wait, on my way to Broadway, to the half-price ticket window—a line I'd never done before. The concept wasn't mine. An accountant at a brokerage firm, a regular customer, was sucking up for a promotion; he wanted to treat the entire executive board to a musical, "Something peppy," he said, but didn't specify. He needed forty tickets for that night. He wired me a thousand dollars to pick up along the way. Now it is rare enough that I wait outdoors, but the coincidence of a sun-dappled afternoon, an undiscovered line, and the proximity of the wait to my home had raised my spirits to the point that, for the first time in two weeks, I did not even glance downstairs at the lamppost before walking out to the elevator.

When the elevator doors slid open, out stepped Detective Lacuna.

He smiled at me, a broad affable smile. The kind of smile designed to put me at ease. Despite the fact that he is a police detective. Despite the fact that he is a large black man with a low voice. "Do you have a minute?"

"Yes."

He glanced down the hall towards my apartment. "May we talk in private?"

"Yes."

Detective Lacuna continued to smile as he ushered me towards the door, as I opened the door and followed him inside. Even as I closed the door behind us, the smile never left his face. "The department has received a tip, an anonymous tip, that you were . . . how shall I say this? That you were *less than frank* with us last month in our homicide investigation."

"Am I a suspect?"

His smile grew even wider. "Do you think you are?"

"I apologize for being less than frank," I said. "It's my nature."

"Then you *were* acquainted with the victim?"

"Slightly," I said.

"Define that."

"I knew him enough to nod at him. But I didn't know his name."

"Is that the truth?"

"Yes."

"Do you know of anyone else who knew him?"

"No," I said.

"Is *that* the truth?"

"As far as I know, yes."

"Were you aware of his comings and goings, even slightly?"

"No," I said. "That's also the truth."

Detective Lacuna continued to smile. He ran his left hand slowly underneath his chin. I was struck by the enormity of his hand; he could have, I believe, clasped my skull and lifted me off the floor.

Finally, he asked, "Is there anything else you'd like to tell me?"

"I think the police do a wonderful job. Often under difficult circumstances."

The smile fled from his face. His hand slipped to his side, and he narrowed his eyes. "Last month, a man was killed. No, make that a *boy*. Somebody killed a boy. Whoever that somebody is, he's still out there. I don't see humor in the situation."

"I don't either," I said; then, I looked down.

"Do you still have the card with my number at the station?"

"Yes," I muttered.

"If you remember something else, anything, even if it seems insignificant, *use it*."

"I will. I promise."

Then he left. I stood motionless and alone.

SEPTEMBER 11:

ezel phoned after midnight and begged me to save him. But he would not tell me what he needed to be saved from, and he bristled when I told him to go back to sleep.

"Just answer me this," he demanded.

"What?" I asked, sleepily.

"If my dick were on a spit, would you pull it off?"

"I suppose, if I had tongs. If I had very long tongs."

"Spare me your lip service," he said. "Yes or no?"

"All right, in that case, yes."

"Then come!" He whispered into the phone an addendum: "It's about Allison Molho."

For a several moments afterwards, I did not move. The words had registered, had even made sense. But there was still too much inertia in my brain to react to them. I shook my head from side to side to shake off what was left of sleep. Zezel had hung up. He knew I was on my way.

The Zezels inhabit a swank co-op on the Upper East Side, near the Guggenheim. How they manage, I don't know, though I suspect she has an inheritance of some sort. No royalties are rolling in from Zezel's unwritten novels; of that much, I am sure. Such matters Zezel and I don't discuss. We even discuss the fact that we do not discuss them, and we call each other *kikes*. Then we laugh since it is a word of which we are both fond, rich as it is with *World-Of-Our-Fathers* charm. When I think of Zezel, sometimes I think of him as "that kike." Riding the Seven Train, before switching to the Uptown Local, I thought, "That kike has gotten himself into a fine mess this time." The smells of the subway were human smells, perspiration and urine. The sounds were metal against metal. The colors were black and gray. Across from me lay a homeless man. He was stretched out across a row of vacant seats, his worldly goods collected in a tattered Macy's bag. The hours after midnight move me to metaphysics, I confess. For what I discerned in the homeless man was faith. Faith in the world as it is, as we perceive it. Faith in a godless world, in a world devoid of metaphysics. To be a bum is to quit the pretense, to accept each moment for what it is and what it isn't. Life in motion. Why bother to plant yourself when nothing takes root? That's what I thought. That's why I avoid the subways at night.

By the time I arrived at Zezel's door, I had worked myself into a state. Now I was full of advice, eager to take an existential stab, to pronounce his fate. I was prepared to judge him for better or worse.

He opened the door as I was about to ring the bell. His face was set in a kind of strained calm—for whose benefit I didn't know. He wrapped his arm around my shoulder and led me into the den. There, Mrs. Zezel awaited us. She sat in a pink bathrobe on a walnut rocking chair. Her eyes were swollen and rubbed to a deep red. The walls of the room were lined with paperback books, stacked seven shelves high, from end to end. Only a pair of reading lamps illuminated the space, and they cast a myriad of shadows. The air was thick with dust. "Behold the man, my love," Zezel said. "The bosomest friend I have in the world. His heart beats in my chest, and mine in his, even as we stand before you. But not only that. For this man is also the very font of truth, an oracle, a proof upon the galleys of the world. Moreover, he has been summoned here, in the wee hours of the morning, at great personal sacrifice, and without complaint: *Ecce!*"

"Sorry for the bother, kiddo," Mrs. Zezel managed.

She sniffled and blew her nose into a handkerchief.

"I don't mind," I said.

"To the gist!" Zezel shouted. "To the gist!"

"Damn it," she shot back. "It's hard enough already."

"What my wife craves," Zezel continued, "or at least what she craves *right now* is certitude. Rare enough in this life. For verily I say that skepticism is the natural state of man. Strip us of our doubts, and by that very act strip us of our freedom. Quiz me no inquisitions! But lay out a foolproof path to heaven, and each man shall live as a saint. Conversely, guarantee that heaven cannot be had, and then it's every man for himself. That is the *sentence* of the situation, my friend. Now favor us with a bit of *solace*."

Mrs. Zezel muttered, "Is my husband involved with another woman?"

"Not to my knowledge," I replied.

"Is that the truth?"

"Yes."

Silence followed.

She daubed her eyes with the handkerchief and grinned. "Hypothetically, if your pal were involved with another woman, and if he dragged you to his house at two in the morning, and if he asked you to lie for him, would you lie for him?"

"Hypothetically?" I asked.

"Hypothetically," she said.

I glanced at Zezel. "I lie for no man."

Zezel walked me downstairs, then the four blocks to the subway station. The air was warm and damp, without the slightest breeze. Neither of us spoke until I was about to descend the steep stairs to the turnstiles.

I turned to him and said, "That felt ... peculiar."

"How so?"

"Peculiar ... I don't know. Peculiar ... bad."

He *tsk-tsk*ed me. "An attack of the *bourgeois?*"

I winced at his words. He clasped my shoulder.

"The police showed up again to ask questions."

"Detective Lacuna?" Zezel asked.

"How did you—?"

"He seems a delightful man, quite inquisitive—a negro if I'm not mistaken."

I stared at him. "*You* phoned in the tip?"

"Does Thoreau shit in the woods?"

"Yes, but—"

"After our conversation two weeks ago," he said, "I felt it my civic duty."

"But why?"

"For your sake, of course. First of all, I'm concerned that your life has become altogether too predictable. There, I've said it. I sense you slipping away, my friend, dissolving like a saltine into the soup of ordinary humanity. Your 'peculiar' feeling a moment ago only confirms my worst fears. Second of all, I would remind you of a certain man beside a certain lamppost. Under the circumstances, I thought it best to finger you. To sheath you, so to speak, within a cloak of protective surveillance. Don't you see? Now that you are a suspect—"

"I'm *not* a suspect."

"Regardless, I have not a doubt that Detective Lacuna will check in on you now and then. So if your bogeyman returns, he is sure to attract the good officer's attention. Unless of course your bogeyman is indeed another detective—in which case their turf war is certain to distract *both* of them from their pursuit of you."

"Ah," I said. And meant it.

Zezel handed me a token. "The least I can do."

The front car of the train I boarded was unoccupied save for me and two Asian girls, high school age from the look of them. Their cheeks were rouged, and their billowy pink sweaters matched; they might have been sisters. The younger-looking one was asleep on the older one's shoulder, the older one asleep on the younger one's head. The sight of them moved me in a much different way from the sight of the homeless man earlier. I stood up from my seat and shuffled towards them, then sat down again across the aisle. There was an allure about them, a dollish purity, that intensified the incongruity of their being on the train at two in the morning. The dewy blackness of their intertwined hairs, their arms folded on their laps, their legs fallen apart as they slept . . . I rose again and sat down next to them. There I remained, silent, motionless, near enough almost to sense the warmth of their bodies, until the train approached Grand Central, where I would transfer to the cross-town Seven Line. Then, at last, I nudged the older girl on the right shoulder. She startled, and the younger one startled as well.

"You were asleep," I said, smiling.

They cowered in their seats and clung to each other. Their eyes were lit up now, their lips taut with fear. There was not a trace of the quiet, the tranquility, of a moment before. As I stood up, they began to tremble. Whether one girl shook the other, or the two of them shook in unison, I could not determine. As the train pulled into the station, I smiled again.

"It's dangerous to fall asleep in the subway," I said. "Especially at this hour. You should avoid it."

The doors slid open.

With their eyes fixed on me every second, I turned and exited the car.

SEPTEMBER 15:

Bit of a chill in the air. A draft has insinuated itself, *ex nihilo*, into my apartment. It runs along the two walls, from the window to the front door, and sweeps across my bare feet as I sit before the computer. It is an annoyance. Not the draft itself, but the thought that the world is different, that something has come lose somewhere which bears upon my existence in a direct way. I am plagued by such randomness. It reminds me how tenuously my feet tread the earth.

Nevertheless, the draft is a minor annoyance. The broad-nosed man is still gone from the lamppost, and he was a major annoyance. More than an annoyance, he was an inconvenience, a two-week enforced hiatus from myself. In order to deal with him, I had to abandon my routine. So I played it safe. The literature I read was sensible, novels by Walter Scott and Hawthorne, verse by Tennyson and Frost; I armed myself with canonical works, which I carried underarm and visible. Every day, for two weeks, I ate meat for dinner. These fragments I have shored against my ruins. For who knew what Broad Nose was after, or when if ever he would be gone? The recollection of him chills me far more than the draft, even now.

But he *is* gone. *Ergo*, Zezel's gambit worked. Or not. But Zezel is my dearest friend, so I will bestow on him the credit, even though I haven't the slightest doubt that his prime motivation in tipping off Lacuna was pure mischief. No doubt Zezel was worried that my life had gotten too predictable; no doubt, too, he considered the possibility that Lacuna would scare off Broad Nose. But these concerns, for Zezel, were secondary and tertiary respectively. No, Zezel is one for mischief. He is a scamp of the first order. When I am not thinking of him as "that kike," I often think of him as "that scamp."

As I stood barefoot at the window, and peered through the blinds at the vacant lamppost, I muttered, "That scamp—I owe him a favor."

SEPTEMBER 17:

Zezel and I met for lunch at the Kosher Deli, my treat, and spoke for many hours of many things. His breath across the table was warmly palpable against the skin of my face. The pitch of his voice would swerve from hush to ejaculation. "That I were a poet!"

"Alas," I said.

"A lass indeed! A bonny lass!"

"She lies over the ocean."

"True, but I lie over the sea."

I squinted at him.

"Think *yesterday's catch*."

"Ah," I nodded. "*The C.*"

"The very nub of my gist."

"But what of your wife?"

"Allison Molho is my wife," he declared. "That other woman is no wife to me."

"Still, you used to love her."

He shook his head. "That was not me. That was another man, another life, for I was born the moment I met the fair Allison."

"Life without history," I said, with envy.

"Presents without pasts."

"*Gelt* without guilt."

"That is the ideal, is it not?"

"But the real world must be addressed," I reminded him.

"For that reason," he said, "I will cleave to the status quo."

I frowned at him. "But what of . . . what of the Good?"

He frowned back. "No, I cannot be bothered. I'm in love!"

He's in love, I spoke to myself. The words seemed to sneer at me, to round themselves off inside my brain. The hazy sky was dimming towards sundown, and I loitered on the corner. Full Pockets had been boarded over two weeks after the bruiséd kid was killed, the regulars scared off by roving foot patrols, and for now the stretch of Eighth Avenue between Forty-Fifth and Forty-Sixth Streets was quiet. I stood before the crooked slats, papered with advertisements for palm readers and underground rock bands. "In love," I muttered aloud. Zezel's use of the word irked me. Curious, since he almost never irks me. But as I loitered on the corner of Forty-Sixth and Eighth, I worked up a considerable irk. The fact that he'd betrayed Mrs. Zezel, that he'd made me a part of his machinations, that he'd forsaken the Good, well, that was just Zezel being Zezel. None of that irked me. Rather, I was irked that he had used the word *love* as his justification. For what had I learned from Holly if not this: Love *inclineth* a man towards the Good. The exemplar, as usual, is scriptural. Love God, sayeth the Sayer-Of-Such-Sayings. Love God with the certitude of madness, with the passion of rapture, with the thrust of revelation. Skip what's left of the Decalogue. Just love God. Ah, but there's the rub. Love God, and the rest follows. Look around. The world is full of Him. No way to foul up His creation except to wound Him. What, wound God? Not me, He's my Luv-ah. Love God, therefore, and the rest falls into place. C'mon, be a saint: Love God!

SEPTEMBER 20:

> Dear M_____,
>
> Your letters have meant so much to me, you don't even know! I mean, you have no idea! The thought that someone out there has been touched by my work has been such a comfort lately. Mr. F. (I just can't call him "Finky" like he wants me to.) says it's only a matter of time before something breaks for me. What scares me is that it might be an arm or a leg! Being a stunt person is for the birds if you ask me. I read Mr. F. your letter about bowling pins and art, but he just kind of laughed. That's not his fault. When you're in the business end of this business, you sometimes forget about the artistic part. So, meanwhile, there's nothing to do but be patient and take my lumps. Actually, I take a lot of hot baths. Which is what I'm doing right now. I hope the edges of the paper don't get steamed.
>
> Last week I read some of your letters to my therapist. I hope you don't mind, but I'd mentioned them to her a few times, and she asked to hear them. She was impressed, I could tell. But then she asked me what I knew about you, and I had to admit I knew just about

nothing. It seems so strange. It seems like I know you very well. But when she asked me for details, I just kind of sat there with my mouth hanging open like a dummy. What an ego-monster I've been! The only thing we ever talk about is me and my problems, never about you. Well, that's going to stop! No ifs, ands or buts. Tell me about yourself in your next letter. I insist! What do you do for a living? Write? Teach? See what you've done? Now I'll have to go on guessing until I hear from you again. At least I know you live in New York City. So you're probably not a surfer dude. (Hah hah!) Are you a butcher? A baker? A candlestick maker? Am I warm? How I *hate* mysteries! Please write back right away, so I can tell my therapist as soon as possible.

Sincerely, Holly

Gentlemen: the corners of the paper *are* steamed. . . .

SEPTEMBER 21:

Dear Holly,

Who am I? What am I? Natural questions, logical questions: if I were a philosopher, I might call them the *qualia.* (Luckily, I'm nothing of the sort.) Still, these are questions I hesitate to address. Not that the answers are difficult or complicated. Quite the reverse, the truth of who I am and what I am is so mundane that I tremble to speak it. Like Sisyphus, I roll my life up a steep incline; the hours weigh into my shoulder, and often it is all I can do to keep the thing going. Who I am is written at the foot of the hill. What I am is momentum. It isn't the answer you want, I know. That, in a moment. This is a preamble, Holly, a citation of nearer and dearer verities prior to the crass particulars. What am I? Here is what I will myself to be: A suit full of dust hung against a blank wall. The planet is going to swallow me in any event. So be it. Dust to dust, no illusions.

But since you've inquired, I will confess that I am in fact a journalist. It's a point of considerable humiliation for me. For what is a journalist except a liar in denial? Truth is the single greatest threat to my livelihood, the sword poised eternally overhead, for if ever the reader asks himself *Should I trust the words?* then I am lost. Never trust the words, Holly! Trust the newsprint, the ink residue on your fingertips, but by no means trust the words! What I contribute pales compared with the ink, as hollow as a sexual metaphor. Words are the substance of me, that by which I subsist. Cast from Eden, I have turned my back on the soil in order to till the *bricolage*. But by what right? Where are the calluses on my hands? Where the groan at the base of my spine? Without such truths, can a man be said to exist? It is only by our pain that we earn our place at the mouth of the void. Between the bookend silences of birth and death, I am a mere echo. That is how I conceive myself—a scratchy echo of the purer silences. The more seductive my words, the closer to death the reader comes. So if indeed death is nothing, then the reader dies between the lines.

Now I have confessed, Holly. Please do not think less of me for what I have told you. Journalist. Liar. Seducer. These are, alas, the particulars of who and what I am. But the particulars do not tell of the possibilities. The particulars are unchanged from last year. Ah, but the possibilities! Last year, there was no possibility that my words would reach you. Now, as your eyes light on these words . . . forgive me, Holly, but of a sudden I feel reborn.

Sincerely yours, etc.

SEPTEMBER 27:

Zezel asked me why I bothered to keep a journal if I refused to allow him to read it. That was last night, after I'd spent a full hour swearing that he hadn't lowered himself in my estimation by his affair with Allison Molho. But in that case, he said, why wouldn't I let him glance at my journal? Only one reason, he had decided: Because my true assessment of him was therein recorded. He was a swine, and there was the truth, encoded in binary intervals, on the hard disk drive.

He had worked himself into a state.

"The journal is for me," I said. "Not for the sake of your conscience. Not for the sake of truth or historical perspective. For no one's sake but mine. For my eyes only, now and forever." I paused and waited for a reaction, but none came, so I added, "Surely you, of all people, would understand that."

"Why me?" he asked, suspiciously.

"Given your past."

His voice began to seethe. "My past?"

"My point is: The journal is for me."

There was another awkward pause.

Then, at last, he smiled. "Well, it sounds too masturbatory for words."

"That too."

"But what about me?"

"You have Allison Molho," I reminded him.

"And whom do you have?" he asked, with bite.

"I have cable TV."

SEPTEMBER 28:

Just when the soil about your feet has begun to settle, when you have hewn your social existence into the hard rock of civilization, your stake is unearthed. I awakened this morning to the new girl, Holly's replacement. She is a sweet-faced thing, all perk and sparkle without a trace of soul. As she bounds across the screen nothing gives, not a hint of give to her flesh. She is too loud for the sunrise.

Then, when I went out for lunch, I passed Detective Lacuna. He smiled at me, the kind of smile intended to reassure me that our encounter was a coincidence. He only smiled. He did not speak to me.

Gentlemen: The truth of the matter is that I knew Aubrey Collins, the bruiséd kid. I took an interest in his doings, in his comings and goings, following our initial exchange on the corner in front of Full Pockets. Once, I discovered him freshly beaten. He was crawling from the very alley in which his body would soon be discovered. He interested me as a case study. Of what, I could not decide. That was the reason I bought him meals and interviewed him on three occasions. During our interviews, we spoke on a range of subjects, and I took copious notes. For the record, his father was a Methodist minister, his mother a phone operator somewhere in the Midwest; he would not reveal the name of the town. He claimed to have been sexually abused by his mother and his uncle, together, an image I could not quite steady in my mind. After he caught the three of them in the act, his father had prayed hard for their souls. The day after he turned seventeen, Aubrey Collins ran off to New York City. As he spoke, he clasped my hand. He *did* believe in God. Why? I asked him. That, he could not answer. When I pressed him, he conceded at last that perhaps he only believed in the word. It was a nice word: *God*. There was more truth than lie in it. He believed in God because the word rang true.

OCTOBER 2:

When I left the apartment this afternoon, Mrs. Zezel awaited me in the lobby of the building, by the mailboxes. She had been there for a half hour, she said, trying to decide whether or not to come upstairs. She knew I was home because I hadn't picked up my mail. But her logic was flawed. What if I'd left before the mail had arrived? Or what if I'd checked the mail on the way out and then left it in the mailbox? She considered these possibilities for a second; then she began to weep. She wept quietly, reluctantly. I stared at her from a distance of several feet until we both felt awkward. By then, she had collected herself.

"He *is* seeing another woman," she whispered. "That much I know."

"Then why have to you come to me?"

"Walk with me, kiddo."

"Where to?"

"How about Washington Square?"

"But that's forty blocks," I said.

She grabbed me by the forearm. "You're in shape. It won't kill you."

As we cut across Forty-Second Street to Fifth Avenue, then turned south towards the park, we didn't speak. The sky was overcast, a milky gray dome of low clouds. The air was thick and cool and moist. It was several minutes after two-o'clock, the pedestrian rush back to work starting to thin out the crowds, but the sidewalks were still jammed. Out of the corner of my eye, I noticed Mrs. Zezel's sporadic glances at passersby. Her eyes lit especially on every pretty woman we passed. Not even once did she glance in my direction.

Then, at last, I turned to her. "What are you looking for?"

"Why don't *you* tell *me*? What *should* I be looking for?"

"Hindsight?"

"I want a name, kiddo. Give me a name."

"I like the name you have."

"Who's kidding whom, kiddo?" She stared at me for a moment, stared into me, and I flinched. As we began to walk again, she continued, "Fair enough. But I've got another question. Did you ever stop and think what a stupid thing a penis is? Apart from its use, I mean. The way it looks. The way it just hangs there. It's kind of a joke if you look at it objectively."

"But it's hard to be objective about it," I said.

She laughed softly. "Touché, kiddo. Touché."

I grinned at her. "I'm still missing your point."

"I don't have one. After all, I'm just a chick."

Several minutes later, we arrived at the park. Mrs. Zezel bought us pretzels and sodas, and we snacked under the great arch of Washington Square. Clustered around the shallow fountain in front of us were NYU students, and scattered among them were a half dozen homeless men, talking to themselves, spitting over their shoulders into the bone dry cement basin of the fountain. Young black men in colorful sneakers moved from cluster to cluster, mumbling the names of their illicit substances. Whenever a policeman wandered by, the pushers withdrew to the wooden benches. Now and then, a squad car drove up on the sidewalk and cruised the concrete paths of the park. Mrs. Zezel and I stood beneath the arch and took it all in. Then she said, "You're his best bud in the world, kiddo. I didn't expect you to rat him out."

"You have a higher opinion of me than I do."

She slid her arm around my waist. "So what do you think?"

I stepped away from her. "What do I think about what?"

"The two of us. You and me. Don't tell me it's never crossed your mind."

"On second thought, maybe you have a lower opinion of me than I do."

"Whose kidding whom, kiddo?" She stepped towards me again, laid her hand on my forearm. "I can get real nasty for a white girl. I'm sure he's told you that."

"Be that as it may—"

"You can trust me. I would never say a thing to him."

"You'd have him on speakerphone as I ejaculated."

Her voice rose. "So what? It's sauce for the goose."

"I'll throw that one back." I grinned again, slightly.

She eyed me with suspicion. "Throw what back?"

"*Sauce for the goose.* It's small fish . . . too easy."

She slapped me hard across the face. "I don't need that crap from you too."

Then she slammed the rest of her pretzel into the garbage and stalked off.

OCTOBER 8:

> Dear M_____,
>
> So I was right! From the very first letter, I knew you were a writer! I knew it! I even told Finky so, but he didn't believe me. He thought you were just another crackpot. (You wouldn't believe some of the mail the girls get!) But I told Finky from the first you were

different. I told him you were sensitive, someone who appreciated the work I had done. So you are a writer after all—what's that saying? You're a *man of letters*. How I admire you for it, for your special gift. No matter what you think, I think writing is an art, and I think artists are special people. We live for others. That must sound so corny! But it's true. If we don't share our gifts with the rest of the world, what good are we? That's the main reason why I'm willing to put up with so much stuff now. So much heartache. Because I know that each hard knock is for a good cause. Not just for fame and fortune. But for the world, so I can share myself. It's only that kind of thinking that gives me the courage to jump out of an airplane. (That's what I did last week. It wasn't so bad, except I landed wrong and sprained my ankle.)

Now you must let me read something of yours. I've googled you dozens of times, but nothing ever comes up. So last week, I went to the library, and I did one of those mega searches, but I still couldn't find you. (I even asked one of the librarians, but she was so snotty to me!) That's the trouble with California. There are no good libraries. Except for the colleges of course. I was going to try UCLA, you know, and do a mega-mega search, but I couldn't get in without an I.D. That really made me mad. Just because I'm not a student, the guard wouldn't let me in. It's not like I needed to borrow a book. All I wanted was to do was a mega-mega search. But that's the way colleges are. I guess that's one of the reasons why I never went to college. So many rules and regulations, and no exceptions. Last year, I went to sign up for night classes, and I must have heard the same words ten times. NO EXCEPTIONS. They told me I had to take dummy math before I took an astronomy course. So I told them all I wanted to do was look at the stars. But then they said the magic words, NO EXCEPTIONS. It was the same story with English. I had to take composition before I could take poetry. But what can you do? It's their school. But I was so discouraged! That was around the time I met Finky. You just can't imagine how happy I was to find someone who finally believed in me! Before that, I was making the rounds, trying to hook up with an agent who could get me speaking parts. But every agent I talked to told me to stick with aerobics. As if that was all I was good for! But Finky was different. The first time he ever met me he said I had star quality. He called it "it." He came up to me in a diner and asked me if I was an actress. He said I had a way about me. At first I thought he was just some creep, but then he gave me his business card. When I told him I was an exercise girl, he asked me why I was wasting my time when it was so obvious that I had "it."

But here I am again, talking about myself. Bad, bad, bad! (I'm slapping my hand.) But seriously I wish you would send me something you wrote. I always like to read between takes when I'm doubling. Usually, I read plays that I might want to act in. Stuff like that. But every now and then I like to sit down with a newspaper. What a thrill it would be to know a journalist! To know that the person who wrote every word, who stuck in every comma and period, knows my name. To know that the same person who wrote about important things also took the time to write to me. To share his gift with me, personally. Oh, please, you *must* send me something! Or else I'll never speak to you again. (Just kidding.) I'll be glad to pay the postage.

Send it as soon as possible.
Anxiously, Holly

OCTOBER 12:

Dear Holly,

How sweet of you to take an interest in my
work, though I must remind you once again that
journalism is just another form of lying. Do not
involve yourself overmuch in it, for it is below you.
Since you seem determined, however, I enclose
a copy of one of my less untrue pieces. (You were
unable to find me through the computer search
because I write under the pen name *Mark Goldblatt*.)
It is a column I was commissioned to write for
Thanksgiving many years ago. I choose this one
out of the lot because I had to fight for it; it almost
did not get published. The editor thought it was too
"downbeat." (His word, Holly, not mine!) Much was
cut from it, much that was decent but "downbeat."
Thus, though I am fond of it, the piece is twice false:
by the words that were cut, and by the words that
remain.

No, Holly, do not involve yourself overmuch with
words. Do as I do. Look towards the Sunrise. For
I have heard the song of an angel in my bedroom.
Holly, it is a song well known to you. Perhaps even
now another collects upon your lips.

Yours always, etc.

Gentlemen, let us be clear on one point: I never meant to
misrepresent myself to such a degree to Holly Servant. But I
have painted myself into a corner and cannot, for the life of me,
conceive an alternative. My own exuberance is to blame. Clearly,
it is my fault, none but mine. Still, how far above myself have I
risen already? She is *anxious* for my response. How, then, can I
disappoint her? The column I forwarded was the very last of

Zezel's entire tabloid career—a last testament, as it were, before he lapsed into silence:

THE PANHANDLER

by Mark Goldblatt

As I strolled up Lexington Avenue last week, with no special destination, I was startled by the sight of a panhandler. He was across the street, standing in front of a pizzeria. The thing that startled me was that he was Asian; I had never seen an Asian panhandler before. Not that I expected never to see one. I hadn't given it a thought until then, the fact that every panhandler I'd ever seen was either black or white or brown. Still, the sight of this man, this Asian man, standing slump-shouldered in front of a pizzeria, caught me by surprise; I decided to watch him for a while.

The first thing I noticed about him, after the fact that he was Asian, was that he was well-dressed for a panhandler. He wore the remnants of a pinstripe suit. He was disheveled, of course; his shirt was tucked in badly in front, and it hung out of the back of his pants, below his jacket, for six inches. His left pant leg was torn off above his ankle. He did not have on socks, or at least he did not have a sock on his left foot. His right pant leg was still intact and fell to the top of his shoe, a perfect fit. The shoes themselves looked pretty good, in need of polish but otherwise presentable.

After a couple of minutes, I decided to cross the street for a closer look. The man appeared to be in his forties. His hair was thick and black, with wisps of gray across his forehead and over his ears.

He clutched a red and white Häagen-Dazs cup to his chest; he didn't put it out for change but relied on passersby to sense his presence. This struck me as a tactical error, as did the fact that his head was bowed. Living in midtown, I've seen enough panhandlers to pick up on the basics. I know eye-contact is crucial. You have to look people straight in the eyes, zero in on the kind-hearted among them, impose a gravity between yourself and them that only can be broken with a coin. Words, in the end, count for less than eye-contact.

Now I don't, as a rule, give cash to panhandlers. I used to give food—until a year ago, when I gave a man in front of Penn Station a can of tuna fish; he hurled it into the back of my neck as I walked away. Since that incident, I can look any panhandler straight in the eyes, gravity neutral, and keep walking.

So I observed the Asian panhandler for several more minutes. He took no notice of me although I now stood perhaps fifteen feet from him and did not move. Once or twice a minute, he lucked out and a passerby dropped a coin into his cup. He would bow abruptly whenever this happened, a habit that underscored the fact that he was an Asian, that he was an Asian panhandler, that he was an oddity.

Eventually, though, I grew self-conscious. As I stood on the sidewalk, unnoticed by him, I was noticed by others. The looks I got were contemptuous—as if it were bad form to stand and stare at a panhandler. So I glanced into the pizzeria and sighted an open stool at a counter just inside the door. From there, I'd be able to watch the Asian panhandler through the storefront window. I walked past him into the pizzeria and bought a sausage slice and a Diet Coke, and I claimed the seat by the window. I observed him for a few more minutes. Finally, he lucked out: Another Asian man, a businessman, emerged from the subway at the corner, spotted the panhandler, marched over and stuffed a five dollar bill into his cup. This was the only donation the panhandler did not acknowledge with a bow. He stared right past his benefactor, out into the street.

As soon as the businessman strode away, the Asian panhandler fished out the five dollar bill from his cup. He held it between his hands momentarily like a miniature flag; then, to my surprise, he turned around and stepped into the pizzeria. The guy behind the counter seemed to know him. He smiled at the him, and he took the five dollar bill without a word spoken between them. Minutes later, he returned with a square Sicilian slice and a large soda on a blue plastic tray. Then he gave him his change, which was a bill and several coins.

The panhandler sat down on a stool at the next counter. He did not begin to eat at first; he only stared at the food on the tray. Then, abruptly, he looked up. He glanced around and behind him. That was when I realized that I wasn't the only one watching him. Seven or eight other patrons averted their eyes. Once he was satisfied that he was no longer the focus of their attention, he turned back around to his pizza. He lifted the slice to his mouth, blew on it, and he took a small bite. Then he set it back down in the plate and took a short sip of soda.

He still had not noticed me as I continued to watch. Because I was seated right in front of him, I had been overlooked by that first glance around and behind. Now, finally, as he set the soda down on the tray, he looked up and our eyes met. So I smiled at him. It's what I've trained myself to do when I cannot avoid another person's eyes. He only smiled back at me, a brief polite smile, then returned to his pizza. I watched him eat for several more minutes, small bites interrupted by sips of soda. During this time, I finished what was left of my own slice. I began to think of other things, work, weekend plans, holiday shopping. I did have errands to run; there was no point in sitting there any longer.

So I stood up.

When I glanced down for a last look at the Asian panhandler, I found him looking up at me. His pizza was half eaten, his soda half empty. He had folded his hands on the table in front of him. His eyes were glowing at the corners, and he started to shake his head side to side. Then he looked at me again. He smiled in a distant way. And then he spoke, in an accent that was barely understandable, "The pizza . . . it's so delicious." When he saw that I had recognized the words, his smile grew broader. "I just love it so much."

His voice trailed off. His shoulders began to quake, and the glow at the corners of his eyes dampened. The full weight of the moment, and of his life, seemed suddenly to bear down on him. He dropped his face into his hands and wept.

The fact that Zezel never wrote another word after "The Panhandler" is tantalizing, or at least it has always struck me as such. I suspect the violins got to him. He swore afterwards that nothing in the piece was true, that, under duress from his editor, he had set out to write a sappy Thanksgiving story. I have never quite believed him. Though he would surely deny it, though he would perhaps stab me in the hand for the mere suggestion, I know what I know: There beats, within Zezel's breast, the heart of a sentimentalist.

Regardless, I am content to claim the piece for mine. Holly is sure to be pleased.

OCTOBER 19:

I t was just after five o'clock in the afternoon. The work crowds were beginning to spill out onto the sidewalks, and I found myself on the corner of Broadway and Fifty-Seventh Street—in their midst. It is a situation I strive to avoid; to be a waiter, caught in a crowd, is like a busman's holiday. I weighed a last-second dash east towards Carnegie Hall, but the flow of bodies had already swept me downtown. Seconds later, I was passing the Ed Sullivan Theater, the double-line of David Letterman's audience turning the corner at Fifty-Fourth. The blur of random lives all about me was claustrophobic, catching me around the heart like a surgeon's hand. Wherever I looked, I saw motion. No single image to latch onto, to sort out, to make sense of. Finally, I shut my eyes. Amid the multitudes, I shut my eyes and continued to walk. Immediately, there were several collisions, shoulder to shoulder collisions that spun me around. But then, after a few moments, nothing. I heard sudden shuffles of footsteps as people lunged from my path, as I was avoided. No one touched me. The fact that my eyes were closed, noticeably closed, had cocooned me. Because I could not see, because I *would not* see, the whole of humankind was making way. Cast yourself from the mountain, challenged Satan: So I had. But I had landed in the arms of my fellow men, and they bore me up.

Bless you, gentlemen, bless you.

OCTOBER 21:

T he Sunrise Workout has evolved into a melancholy ritual. Bess, my favorite after Holly Servant, has left the program as well. Nicole appears irregularly. The show has been overhauled, a new red and white striped backdrop hung behind the girls. Peppermint candy, before breakfast! There is new, louder music too. Holly's voice used to be a summoning, a call from one dream to another. The new faces are too young, usurpers of the morning's quiet; their voices are like scratch codes.

Nevertheless, I'll not surrender the hardness of my stomach to such misfortune. It is impressive, the hardness of my stomach, as I stand before the mirror. It is like tire rubber, rippled enough to glisten at the end of the workout. To enhance the effect, I shave it. Now the sweat forms a network of rivulets, each of which defines a muscle group. I linger before the mirror; I am Narcissus. But I'll not fall in. There are too many reasons to keep my powder dry.

OCTOBER 22:

Zezel asked me to meet him at high noon in front of the Kosher Deli. "To touch base," he stated. "To sift among the softball ruins of time, and to spank the Clincher of truth." He awaited me in the drizzle, and his skin glowed like a washed apple. Then he embraced me, held me to his breast for a long time. Then, at last, he said, "Here is my heart!"

I smiled at him. "What heart?"

"*Et tu, mon frère?*"

"Let us not mix our Romances."

"Sound advice . . . good shtick."

"No shtick," I said.

"No shtick?"

"Not for the time being."

"Not even a wee shtick?" he pleaded. "What if we spoke softly and pretended? It's not the size of the shtick that matters. It's how you present it. That's what my dear old dam always told me. She used to bathe me back then—"

"Uncle," I said.

"He and my mother? The two of them? I never suspected." He rolled the thought over in his mind, then stepped back indignantly. "No! I am not Prince Hamlet, nor was meant to be."

"You'll never have to feign madness for my sake."

"*Exeunt omnes.*" He pulled open the door to the deli, and I followed him inside.

But as we were served, his mood altered. He spoke to me about

Allison Molho in a slow and sober voice, a baritone in search of a melody, and I could barely recognize his face. It seemed twisted and misshaped by emotion, taut about the jowls, drawn in at the lips. He wasn't ugly, but he was painful to look at. He ate less and less, talked more and more. His hot open roast beef sandwich grew cold. "Do you recall when we used to play ball in Central Park?" he said. "The world was so much younger then, and we played softball on the Great Lawn. We would sun ourselves like reptiles on the shale boulders behind the museum. Surely, *mon frère*, you must remember! We would sun ourselves and leer at the girls who passed by."

"Daphne," I said. "We'd call them Daphne."

"Then you *do* remember!" he cried, happily.

I nodded. "Forever halcyon. Forever yore."

"Then you must remember how Daphne would rush past on rollerblades, or on a bicycle, or even on foot, and how we would watch her crack-an-egg-on-it ass jiggle across the rough stretches of asphalt."

"The canvas runneth over," I declared.

"Then fix it fast in your mind," he said. "For now, at long last, I will confess with my confession: I never saw her. Though we sunned and leered and lingered long, I never once saw Daphne."

"Myopia?"

"Quite the reverse," he replied. "The problem was visionary. What I saw was a dollar sign where her cunt would be."

"No euphemisms?" I asked.

"Do you see what love has wrought? I've no time for euphemisms!" He slammed his fist down on the table; there was a ripple effect in his glass of cream soda. "So I reiterate, I never once saw Daphne—*until now*. For Allison is Daphne, and Daphne is Allison. Don't you see what I'm saying? Whatever else the world has withheld, now at last I've come across and come into my own Daphne!"

"Now, at last, you've shtuck it to her."

"Just so." His pale skin was radiant.

"What of your wife?"

"What of her?"

"Left holding the shtick?"

"So it would seem. Still, what's to be done? The heart has

its own . . . "

 "Its own what?" I asked.

 "It's own . . . "

 "Yes?"

 Panic came into his eyes. "I can't remember."

 "Agenda? The heart has its own agenda?"

 He shook his head.

 "Its own . . . logic?"

 "No." He winced.

 "Society?"

 "No, that's the soul."

 "Dickinson?"

 "Shtick!" he cried.

 "What?"

 "The heart has its own shtick."

 "Ah," I said.

OCTOBER 26:

The gaunt woman in Room 21B4 steadied my wrist with less force than her usual vice grip as she drew blood this afternoon, a breakthrough in our relationship. Or so it seemed to me. There was silence after the deed, after the prick itself, silence in place of the standard questions, as the scarlet trickle began to fill the vial. I sensed a delicate sadness through her fingertips.

 "It must be a lonely calling—science, I mean."

 She arched her eyebrows. "What would you know about it?"

 "Science? Or loneliness?"

 "What would you know about either one?"

 "I know that water freezes at 32 degrees," I responded.

 She grinned at me. "Very impressive. What's my name?"

 "Your name?"

 "It's your seventh visit. You haven't even asked my name."

 "I didn't want to trespass," I said.

 "Trespass on what?"

 "The principle of objectivity, of detachment. You know, scientific method."

"I don't see how the study would be compromised if I told you my name."

"All right," I said.

She released my wrist and capped the vial; then she gave me a bandage as she stored the vial in the miniature refrigerator built into the bottom drawer of the desk. She snapped off her disposable elastic gloves and thrust her bare right hand over the desk.

"Penelope Estes," she said.

I shook her hand.

"My partner and I quarreled last night," she said. "Sorry, I've never been able to conceal things."

"Your *partner*."

"Yes."

"You and your *partner* quarreled."

"Yes."

"About what?" I inquired.

"The usual. Families. The future."

"You and your *partner*."

"Do you have a problem with the word?"

"I know many partners, both animated and live action."

"Such as?"

"Heckle and Jeckle. Jekyll and Hyde."

"What about in real life?"

"The Lone Ranger and Tonto?"

"That's not real life," she said.

"Dorothy and Toto? Wilbur and Mr. Ed?"

She shook her head. *"Real life."*

"Sacco and Vanzetti? Leopold and Loeb?"

"Do you know them personally?"

"Just what I read in the movies."

"What I mean by my *partner* is my *lover.*"

"I *said* Wilbur and Mr. Ed!"

"I quarreled with my lover," she stated.

"What was the cause?"

"Her friends keep trying to set her up with men. I think she should be honest with them. But she's afraid the truth will get back to her parents." Penelope Estes paused, then added, "She's from Ohio."

"Ah." I nodded my head.

She sighed. "I don't know what to do. Maybe I'm being unreasonable."

I continued to nod.

"They're her *parents*, I mean—"

"You could wait for them to die. They will, you know. They always do."

"Are your parents dead?"

"My mother died of me."

"In other words, she died in childbirth."

"So the story goes," I said.

"I've started to make sense of your double-talk."

"It's only double-talk half the time."

"What about your father?" Penelope Estes asked.

"The old Laius himself!"

"Is he dead too?"

"Years ago. Where three roads meet."

"Were you close to him?"

"The apple doesn't fall far from the ladder."

"Don't you mean the tree?"

"If the tree falls, the ladder goes down with it."

"How do I step off the carousel?" she asked.

I smiled at her. "You just wait until it stops."

When I arrived home, I found a note slipped under the door. It had the look of a ransom note, lettered with cut-out characters from magazines and newspapers, pasted in uneven lines across a sheet of construction paper. It read:

I KNOW WHO KILLED AUBREY COLLINS

There were no demands, no punctuation, not even an ellipsis to indicate more would follow. I held the sheet of paper up to the sunlight that came through the window. The craftsmanship was poor; the letters were crooked and unevenly spaced, and the last two words, "Aubrey" and "Collins," were crammed together. In fact, had I not realized the sense of the note, I might have read it as

i kn OwwHo kiLLed aubreYcoLLins

But I did realize the sense of the note, and I began to tremble.

OCTOBER 27:

Detective Lacuna sat on a cracked wooden chair behind a rusted metal desk piled high with paperwork. The desk itself was tucked into a corner cubicle at the rear of the precinct. He looked up as I peered around the edge of the cubicle. It took a second for him to recognize me, but when he did, his expression changed. The beginnings of a smile formed at the corners of his mouth, and he leaned back. The wooden chair creaked loudly.

"I found this under my door."

I handed him the note and sat down on the metal chair next to the desk. He read the words several times; then he held the construction paper up to the stark overhead light. Finally, he shrugged and passed the note back to me. He said nothing.

"What do you make of it?" I asked.

"I don't know what to make of it. I don't know what to make of *you*."

"Shouldn't you dust it for fingerprints?"

"Whose would I find?" he responded.

"I don't have a clue."

"No," he said, "you *do* have a clue. You're holding it in your hand."

"I don't know who killed Aubrey Collins."

"Apparently, somebody thinks you do."

"That's not much of a comfort," I said.

Detective Lacuna leaned forward and set his elbows on the rusted metal desk. The faint smile persisted on his face. He folded his two large hands in front of his face and stared at them. He seemed on the verge of speaking for a long time, an unnaturally long time. Then, at last, he said, "Two questions come to mind. First, who wrote the note? Second, why did whoever wrote it leave it under you door? Now, you tell me you don't know the answer to the first question—and I believe you. But I'm having a hard time believing that you don't know why it wound up under your door."

Even as he spoke, though, I had suddenly solved both questions. Zezel was the author of the note, and he'd left it under my door for the very reason that he knew I would panic and bring it to Detective Lacuna. *That scamp*, I thought, as I watched the detective's lips form the words "under your door."

"I've told you all I know," I said. Then I stood up.

"May I keep the note?" Detective Lacuna asked.

I hesitated for an instant but then gave it to him.

If he traces it back to that scamp, I thought, *it will serve both of them right.*

OCTOBER 31:

The telephone hangs soundlessly on the wall, and the mailbox is vacant. It is too cold for an afternoon walk, but if I had a plausible destination I would venture out regardless. Not a chance. So I sit . . . now in front of the window, now in front of the computer, soon in front of the lunch I have laid out for myself. So I sit, and I await nothing.

Holly, where are you? It's been three weeks.

Just as I sat down to lunch, a cockroach skidded to a sudden halt on the kitchen counter. Out of the corner of my eye I noticed him, but I made no move. He froze in his position, and I froze in mine. For well over a minute, neither of us moved. He remained motionless four feet away, at the precise center of the Formica counter. He could not have chosen a worse spot. Still, he waited, and I waited. Had I removed my glance, returned to my lunch, I felt certain he would have scurried in the direction of the nearest crack. But I had fixed him in my sight, had fixed him *by* my sight, and he had fixed me in and by his, and we were at an impasse.

As I felt for the napkin next to my sandwich, I expected him to break for the wall. Had he bolted at that instant, he might have saved himself since the napkin was not where I first reached for it but half a foot away. He did not however. His best instincts had deserted him, and he appeared at that moment transcendent, risen above and sunken below his own nature. That was what I thought as I stood up from the table.

He remained transfixed even as I loomed above him, even as the shadow of the napkin fell over him. The shadow of death. With that thought, I found myself unable to bring down the weight of my fist behind the napkin. Not as long as he kept still. What I needed was for him to waver, to break for safety. I needed the electric spark of action in order to react. I could not kill him except spontaneously. I withdrew the hand with the napkin and, without taking my eyes from him, pulled open the counter drawer. He must have felt the rumble underneath him, but he still did not move. After several seconds, I fished out an old tin of lighter fluid and brought it to a point above him. Now I dared not remove my glance from him. I felt for the plastic cap and snapped it back, then inverted the tin. Drop by drop, I bled a perfect circle of lighter fluid around him. With each drop, I thought he must make his break. But still he did not move.

At the far end of the counter lay a box of oven matches. As I stretched for it, the warm embarrassment of what I was about to do, of what I had done already, crept across my face: I was blushing as I drew out a single match and struck it against the edge of the box. As the match fell towards the counter, the roach flinched but did not run. He was at once surrounded by a circle of fire, still unharmed in the center, as I stepped back to watch. He spun in every direction, approached the flames twice, and then at last hurtled through. But his legs caught in the molten Formica, half in half out, before the gravity of the flames drew him back to their crackling embrace.

The counter is ruined but, for the moment, too expensive to resurface.

NOVEMBER 1:

hen I returned home from a job at the courthouse, I found another note slipped under my door. It read:

THE PRICE OF SILENCE: $37.93

That scamp!

NOVEMBER 3:

ezel telephoned to warn me that he and Mrs. Zezel were in the neighborhood and were about to drop in. He spoke in a rapid whisper that was difficult to make out amid the background of street noise. What I gathered was this: He feared that his wife was suffering some sort of breakdown, or else that she had planned his assassination (his word) for that very afternoon, and he swore that he was not paranoid, that he had his reasons. Then he swore at the world, into the phone.

As I collected up old newspapers from the floor, I swore at the morning.

Several minutes later, the two of them arrived at the door, arm in arm. Mrs. Zezel indeed had the trodden-eyed look of nervous collapse about her, but then she shot me a glance of ice cold sanity to acknowledge our last conversation in Washington Square Park. Whatever she was up to with Zezel, there was calculation behind it. Wedded at the hip, the two of them sat down on the couch. They held hands and smiled as I put up water for instant coffee.

"This is a swell couch," Mrs. Zezel called to me. "It's the kind of couch you can build a room around. It's more than swell. It's ... *lovely.*"

"And so say all of us!" Zezel added.

"Thank you," I called back to them.

Zezel inquired, "So have you plans?"

I leaned out of the kitchen. "Plans for what?"

"To build a room," he said. "To build a lovely room around this lovely couch. So that in the future, when I bring my lovely wife to sit upon your lovely couch, she will be surrounded on every side by ever lovelier and lovelier loveliness."

"No," I said. "I have no plans."

"More's the pity!"

"Is this a bad time, kiddo?" Mrs. Zezel called.

"But love of my life," her husband said, "between good friends there are no bad times —"

"That's a crock of hooey," she cut him off. "Even between good friends, there are bad times. Of course kiddo is going to be kiddo and tell us how happy he is we dropped by, but if it's a bad time, then we ought to leave."

I returned with three cups of brown powder on a plastic tray.

"*Good* friends . . . *bad* times . . . surely, my dear, you have embraced a paradox."

"All right, forget I said *bad* times. *Less fortunate* times. Between good friends, there are *less fortunate* times. So cut me a little slack, will you?"

"Do you see how clever my wife is?" Zezel said. "She's been here not five minutes, and already she has resolved her paradox. Squared her circle, so to speak. Is she not the Peg-O'-My-Heart?"

Their words were like bullets aimed at each other's faces: I needn't have been in the room. Their lips worked over each syllable, wrapped around each vowel with a slow and bitter precision. As I waited for the kettle on the stove to whistle, the tension in the room was as thick as blood.

When the whistle came, I hopped to it.

The coffee served to quiet them. They drank in discrete sips, both of them, and Zezel ran his hand up and down his wife's thigh. Only one time did his eyes meet mine; he glanced down at his hand on her lap, and then he rolled his eyes toward the ceiling as though to underscore his distaste at where his hand rested. It was a look I dared not acknowledge.

Finally, she said to me, "So how goes the career?"

"Time is money," I replied.

"Strangely, however, not the reverse," Zezel said.

She turned towards him. "How do you figure that?"

"The equation, my dearest; I refer to the equation."

"Time is money?"

"Therefore, one would infer, money must be time," Zezel said. "But how often is it the case that the *haves* of the world have not world enough and time!"

"It's what keeps me in business," I agreed.

"I *hate* being in a room with the two of you!" she shouted abruptly. She began to stand up, but Zezel tightened his grip on her thigh and did not allow her to rise. After a second effort, she wheeled about and slapped him hard across the face. He responded by hurling his body onto her. For several moments, they struggled on the couch. Then he pinned her arms at her sides, and she lay still. They stared into one another's eyes with ferocious venom.

Then, suddenly, they began to kiss.

"I'll leave you two alone for a while," I said, finishing my instant coffee.

And so I did.

NOVEMBER 9:

Dear M_____,

Thank you so much for your beautiful newspaper article. It was so sad about that Chinese man, the way he had to beg for money to buy a piece of pizza. It just makes me want to cry when I think about it. How can people just walk past another human being who is hungry for food? I see that kind of thing all the time in downtown L.A.—Mexican families, kids and all, camped out on the sidewalks. So I give them what I can, a quarter or two. Or, if I just got paid, maybe a dollar. But then they're still there the next day, on the same corner, week after week. It's like nothing changes. It's just so sad. Sometimes, I want to just grab someone, maybe a politician, I want to just grab him by the arm and say, "Look at that!" The United States is supposed to be the richest country in the world. But people are starving in the streets! How can that be? But just listen to me! Like I'm the president or something! Like people are going to sit back and wait for Holly Servant to tell them what's wrong with the world!

But that's just me, I guess. Full of opinions. My mouth is my downfall. That's what Finky tells me, and he should know. So we spend hours and hours going over what I should say if we meet a producer at a party. "The less the better," is what Finky says. But if I have to talk at all, we've got a list of safe subjects—you know, where it would be hard to put my foot in my mouth. I'm allowed to talk about health food and exercise and sex, but not about movies or television or acting. Finky likes it best when I talk about sex because, he says, they're not listening anyway. I'm not sure what he means by that. Maybe just that a pretty girl can get away with a lot as long as she talks dirty. But that's not me, I tell him. Don't get me wrong. I'm no prude. I like sex as much as the next gal. But I don't like to talk about it. What's the point?

Anyway, things have been going okay here, I guess. I even got to say a line on *General Hospital*. But then I died. But Finky swears that if the show gets enough mail, I could come back as another character. What a strange thing to think you can die and come back as somebody else! Do you believe in that sort of thing? (I do, kind of.) What do you believe in?

God, it feels so good to talk about things! Serious things, like politics and religion. It's like I have all these ideas bottled up inside me and no one to pop the cork! But Finky knows best. He did get me that line on G.H.

Well, I've got to run now. I've got a call back for a cop show pilot. Thanks again for your article.

love, Holly

P.S. I'm going to be in New York for Christmas.
Would you like to get together?

NOVEMBER 10:

O f course, Christmas! Christmas, Gentlemen—*Felix culpa*, if ever there was one. Cast me from the Garden towards the shadow of the Cross if therein lies deliverance. Now, I celebrate the litany of my transgressions for the glorious redemption won. 'Tis the season to deck the halls, for, unless I am mistaken, I detect a new star in the heavens! Now is the nativity of my love, of my desire, of my life's work. Glory to the newborn king.

Gentlemen: a most fortunate fall indeed!

NOVEMBER 11:

Dearest Holly,

Am I blessed by the prospect of Christmas? Is the earth blessed by the lighting snow? Trampled and begrimed, I am the cold mud of November. But now I quicken with anticipation: The sign of the sugarplum princess has appeared above the dirge of night. She will reign over me, cast her sweetest smile across the horizon, and the world will be rendered immaculate yet again. By the frost of her breath, the air will be cleansed. By the whites of her eyes, every evil will be undone.

Holly, I confess: The thought of you in New York for Christmas moves me to new shades of purple. Shall we take a carriage ride in Central Park? By all means, call upon me Christmas Eve! (Then you will know me from Adam!) It has been a dream of mine for as long as I can remember to ride a horse-drawn carriage on Christmas Eve. I cannot think of another soul to share such a night with. There are so few of us dreamers left! So few of us who pursue an ideal no matter the hardship. No matter the consequence. The dreamer stands naked upon the stage of the wide world—and if the people should recoil in disgust, cast him out from the theater, still he would continue to dream. Even now, if I stand naked, what of it? If I rant and rave without a script, in a voice that is my own, will the audience even listen? Or am I at last alone with my words? Until I heard your voice, I thought so. Until you cued me to the dawn, I tossed clever one-liners off the edge of the world. But now I know there is a more resonant truth, a truth of music, of breaths drawn in unison, of voices lifted in harmony. Each moment, now, a chord struck against the evil of silence.

Let us carol together, Holly!

yours, devotedly, etc.

NOVEMBER 14:

Penelope Estes, the gaunt woman in Room 21B4, telephoned to ask why I'd missed the last two-week interval. I told her the truth: The appointment had skipped my mind. (It fell on the very day I received Holly's letter.) I apologized at length and then arranged to see her in the afternoon.

How could I have known the wonders that awaited?

Determined to show my contrition, I arrived on the twenty-first floor a half hour before I was scheduled. The elevator doors parted, and I walked in the direction Room 21B4. The hall was familiar to me now, the abstract silk-screens that lined the walls, the clusters of aquamarine lounge furniture, the checkerboard carpet. Nothing was out of the ordinary. But then at once I heard a series of sounds: first, the swinging of a door on its hinge; second, the *thwang* of a latch spring; finally, a muted moan. Tingling with curiosity, I realized that the sounds had come from Room 21B4.

Now I stood in front of the door and listened. There were more sounds, the sliding of a chair, then another chair, the whisper of voices, then a long low sigh. I laid hold of the cool brass doorknob and twisted it slightly to the right. It gave soundlessly. The door slid open several inches.

Now I saw Penelope Estes. She was lying on her back, lying across the desk, lying in the arms of another woman. The two of them were oblivious to me, to the fact that the door had slid open, to the fact that they were being observed—even as I stepped into the room. I could not make out the face of the second woman; it was partially obscured by a haphazard waterfall of blond hair. They were pressed together now, the two slender bodies, their limbs intertwined, the blond streams mingling with the brunette mass; I took another step towards the women. Their kisses were airy and delicate, almost silent. Their clothes were parted at the breasts and genitals. As I watched, the blond woman lifted a hardcover book from an open drawer on the far side of the desk and brought it between the legs of Penelope Estes. The touch of the book elicited another loud sigh.

How I longed to know the title of that book!

Penelope Estes now took the blond woman by the back of her head, her fingers twisting in strands of blond hair, and guided her head down towards her nether parts; I lost the book for a moment, then caught sight of it again below the curved flesh of her thighs. It seemed to dance up and down, the book, a rhythmical dance, and soon the rhythm had overcome the two women, their breaths, their kisses, their caresses. Eventually, the book dropped to the floor with a loud thud.

"I'll get it," I said.

They lurched apart. The second woman was sent backwards off the end of the desk as Penelope Estes pulled her arms to her knees and curled up into a tight hunch. As the second woman crawled behind the desk, I picked up the book from the floor and peeked at the title: *Masterpieces of the Western World in Digest Form, Volume Two.* Then I handed the book to Penelope Estes.

She took the book and slammed it down onto the desk.

"What are you doing here?" she shouted.

"We have an appointment. Did I come at a bad time?"

"Get out!"

I backed out of Room 21B4 and closed the door behind me. Then I waited in front of the door for several minutes. There were frantic words inside the office, but I made an effort not to overhear them. Finally, the blond woman emerged. She was pretty in a delicate sort of way, fine-featured, hazel eyed; her blouse was still slightly rumpled as she stepped past me. She paused only long enough to glare.

I knocked on the door.

"All right," Penelope Estes called to me.

She was seated as usual behind the desk, in her green lab smock, as I stepped into Room 21B4. "Didn't your mother ever teach you to knock?"

"My mother died of me," I said.

"Yes, I remember." Despite herself, she began to smile. "You still should have knocked."

"So that was your partner?"

"Yes."

"She's very pretty."

"I think so."

"As partners go, I mean."

She continued to smile.

"I especially admired her hair."

"I'll mention that to her tonight."

"Does the carpet match the drapes?" I asked.

She tilted her head to the side. "What?"

"Is she a natural blond?"

Penelope Estes laughed loudly. "That's a new one!"

"Well?"

She gave one last sigh, then shut her eyes and shook her head. When she opened her eyes again, her expression was blank. She reached across the desk and grasped me by the wrist. "Have you experienced effects?"

"None that I know of," I said.

"Depression?"

"No."

"Euphoria?"

"No."

"Paranoia?"

"Nothing beyond the usual."

NOVEMBER 21:

The first snow of the season, a bare whisper of snow, falls outside the window. It is so faint that had I not opened the window for a breath of air, I might have overlooked it. Now, as the cold breeze rushes through the window, the hairs on my arm rise up like a winter forest.

NOVEMBER 26:

Zezel suggested a change of venue for lunch: Chinatown. Change for change's sake was his rationale, a discreet peek over the rut's edge. He suggested a restaurant whose name contained many vowels. He'd eaten there the week before with Allison Molho, and he swore by the food. "It's a positive aphrodisiac, on my word."

"You'll still respect me after the pork?"

"I don't respect you now," he replied.

So we arranged to meet at one o'clock—which turned out to be an error. The sidewalks were a tight huddle of dark overcoats, barely moving against the high plexiglass storefronts. There were shouts and shoves as people struggled to reach appointments, the blare of car horns and the screech of brakes as pedestrians made diagonal dashes across intersections. I arrived ten minutes late, ten minutes before Zezel. As we entered the restaurant, I heard a familiar voice call out my name. Detective Lacuna rose from a rear table and motioned us towards him. Before I could react, Zezel was on his way. I followed him, reluctantly, and, even more reluctantly, I introduced the two of them.

Lacuna smiled at Zezel and said, "That's an unusual name, isn't it?"

"On the contrary," Zezel replied. "Nothing could be more mundane. I've had it since the very moment I was born—if my mother is to be believed. I see no reason to *dis*believe her on this account. Even though, as we are all aware, a mother is not always to be trusted."

"You boys want to sit down?" Lacuna asked.

No sooner were the words spoken than Zezel was seated next to the detective. "Do you come here often?"

"Three times a week," he said, nodding. "Best lo mein in the city. None of that chopstick bullshit either. Silverware's already on the table. You don't have to ask for it special. I like that."

So: The coincidence was no coincidence. Zezel had picked the restaurant, the day, and the time. I should have been suspicious. He must have noticed Lacuna the week before, with Allison Molho, and planned a "chance" encounter. Now I muttered underneath my breath: *That kike!*

Zezel asked, "How goes the investigation?"

"What investigation?" the detective said.

"I speak of the Collins case. Murder most foul."

Lacuna glared at me, then turned back to Zezel. "It's moving along."

"I have a theory of my own—"

I cut him off. "No one is interested—"

The detective patted my hand. "No, let the man speak. *I'm* interested."

Zezel smiled. "According to the newspaper accounts, no one in the vicinity heard a struggle that night. Therefore, I speculate that the victim must have been acquainted with his killer."

"Your theory has a couple of flaws," Lacuna stated. "The fact that no one *heard* a struggle doesn't mean that no struggle took place. Given the neighborhood and time of night, it might mean that no one was close enough to hear a struggle, or it might mean that somebody heard a struggle but doesn't want to come forward and talk about it because he was where he shouldn't have been."

"Interesting," Zezel nodded.

Just then, the Chinese waiter arrived. He was young, the approximate age of Aubrey Collins, with close cropped hair and narrow shoulders. He bowed as he wrote down our orders and then retreated to the kitchen.

"As it happens," Zezel continued, "I have a suspect in mind."

"Do you?" Lacuna said skeptically.

"Indeed I do."

I tried to kick Zezel under the table but caught the wood support beam instead. The cups of tea rippled with the impact.

"As I envision the moment," Zezel said, "Death incarnate descends upon Collins in the subtle crack between twilight and dawn. Perhaps for a daily dose of mortal terror, or perhaps only for sport. But rather than fall to his knees in dread, Collins falls to his knees in readiness. He doggies up to the very footfall of Death, parts the black robe in front of him, parts his lips in vain thirst. But my imagination fails at this point."

"Too bad," Lacuna said.

After we were served, I raised my eyes from my plate only as necessary. Clatter from the kitchen filled the lack of conversation. The waiters grouped now and then near our table and sorted out orders in confused and urgent tones.

The steam from my meal was laced with spices and black peppers, and I began to sweat. The meat itself was tough but seductive. I could not eat it fast.

Finally, Zezel turned to Lacuna and said, "May I ask a question?"

"I'm not promising I'll answer, but go ahead and ask."

"Do you consider yourself a hero?"

"No, I don't," Lacuna replied.

"Not even a whisper of hubris?"

"I don't follow."

"Oedipus, for example, thought himself master of his own fate. Now of course the gods thought otherwise."

"No one is master of his own fate," Lacuna insisted. "Too much is left to chance."

"Precisely!" Zezel said. "But in such hubris we also glimpse Oedipus the hero."

"As I recall the story, doesn't he kill his father and fuck his mother? That's not my idea of a hero."

"But consider what he dared," Zezel said. "The oracle spake unto him his future, and he begged to differ. He set out from Corinth in order that his future never find him. What balls! How unlike the rest of us who mill about the hero, strophing and anti-strophing, awaiting our destinies. Take our mutual friend over here."

Now at last I glanced up.

"Here is the stuff of the Chorus," Zezel continued. "The sort of fellow who takes the oracle at its word, who makes do. The sort of fellow who picks flowers for mommie dearest on the way back from Delphi. Why dispute the gods? he thinks to himself. Not a trace of hubris here!"

"You keep using that word, *hubris*—"

"It's what we academics call an excess of pride. Haven't you read your *Cliffs Notes?*"

The detective grinned. "Never was much of a scholar. But I do study human nature."

"To be sure," Zezel said. "Because you are a man of action, a doer, a mover and a shaker. That's the very reason I consider you a hero. *My* hero. The paragon of animals. I think I speak for my friend also in this regard. By his smiling he seems to say so."

"Man delights not me," I said, despite myself, "nor woman neither."

"Am I missing something?" Lacuna asked.

"Never!" Zezel responded. "For a hero leaves no stone unturned, nor turd unstoned, in his quest for the truth. To return to Oedipus, is it not his very determination to bring the truth to light that causes his downfall? Consider: He might have halted his investigation into the murder at any point as the composite photo took on a more and more noble aspect. He might have backed off, shrugged his shoulders for the sake of the crowd, then retreated to the palace and allowed the plague to ravage Thebes. Yet he didn't. He followed through. He couldn't help but do so because he was a hero."

"So what's your point?"

"There is no point," Zezel stated. "I was just making conversation, just pointless conversation."

Detective Lacuna shook his head and continued his meal.

NOVEMBER 30:

Zezel called from a public phone just before dawn to update me on his liaison with Allison Molho. I grew certain I was awake only as he began to describe the grains and odor of her vagina:

"How unlike a rose," he said. "But a flower nevertheless. Perhaps a water lily, risen like a shrine above the pond scum, singular and fragrant. For I have worshipped there, dear friend. I have drowned upon my knees in homage. What filled my mouth was cool and saline, essence of yesterday's catch."

"Too early," I muttered.

"But Woman is the sudden past," he said. "The sooner we fix her in our minds, the closer we come to the truth. Where Man points forward, one eye forever towards the future, Woman recedes. We come to her in our most collective memories. As we near her, we recollect the millennia—not as ourselves but as Otherness personified. We lose our legs and start to swim. We grope for land, for substance, but our hands are senseless, grown over with scales."

DECEMBER 4:

> Dear M_____,
>
> Everything is set for New York! Or as I call it the Big Apple. Finky has already lined up a laundry commercial for the week starting the twenty-first, and the shoot shouldn't take more than two days. For sure, not past Christmas Eve. After that, my time is my own. So keep that carriage ride open for me if you can. Speak to you soon. (What does your voice sound like I wonder!)
>
> love, Holly

Do not think, gentlemen, I have failed to notice the signature at the close of her last two letters. What is crucial is to stay within myself, to keep a correct perspective. Holly Servant does not love me. That is not possible. But her nature is such that a kind of love follows, as a matter of course, once her emotions are roused. That is the reason I selected Zezel's final column. His sentimental words have poked her in the heart, and she is without the styptic of cynicism; she cannot help but bleed.

DECEMBER 5:

rs. Zezel is asleep on the kitchen counter. The story of how she got there, I'll not recount in detail. (Gentlemen do not dwell on such particulars.) What matters is that *I* left her there, I myself: I have betrayed Holly Servant. That, and I've cuckolded Zezel, the dearest friend I have ever known.

But I am no martyr. No, I'll not bear the onus of the evil deed alone. For I did not appear at her door, but she at mine. Nor did I wet her sleeve with my tears. The warmth of her sudden tears softened the stiffness of my mood, loosened the stiff musculature of my shoulders. I held her close. That is how it began. What matters is that it ended on the kitchen counter.

Of the hundred images and sensations of last night, I'll share only these few: Her dark hair spread like a hoop skirt against the Formica; the gentle hum of the refrigerator just behind us; the faint suck and slither of her back as she arched into me, as she wriggled like an eel on a hook. I said nothing to her the entire time, and what she said to me came to nothing. She called me *honey* and *baby* and *lover*, and when it was over, she called me a son-of-a-bitch.

Only the last was spoken with the slightest affection.

She also told me that I tasted sweeter than any man she'd ever been with. It took me a moment to figure out what she meant: I thought, at first, she meant my lips. They were swollen from her kisses. But then I realized she meant my semen—to which she had returned over and over in the course of the night. "You're like caramel, baby," she muttered. No one had ever mentioned that before, and afterwards I was troubled by the observation. As she slept on the kitchen counter, I began to worry. The first thought I had was diabetes—a Zezelian thought if ever there was one. So I tiptoed into the bathroom and fished out the roll of Tes-Tape Zezel had presented me when I turned twenty-one. ("To life!" he said, which was his entire toast.) For a full minute, I held my breath as the yellow strip stayed yellow, and then with a sigh I dumped the urine into the toilet and tossed the cup into the garbage. Then I sat down on the lid of the bowl and stared straight ahead. If not blood sugar, how to account for the sweetness? So I shut my eyes and imagined Holly Servant. She sat alone in the bathtub, smiling at me. Her eyes cut like jewels through the clouded air as the bathwater lapped against the small of her back, as perspiration gathered under her slender arms. She spoke words I could not hear. Now I trembled. The sensation left my face, and I cupped my palms. What I tasted thereafter was warm but not sweet, the essence of myself. To know this, after the night before, I ached.

When at last Mrs. Zezel climbed down off the kitchen counter, she put up two mugs of instant coffee. She hummed as she waited for the water to boil, but she did not call out to me. So I crept to the edge of the kitchen and peered around the corner. She was naked. She rifled through the kitchen drawers—in search of nothing it seemed. She only opened and shut each drawer, one after another, as if taking stock. She found nothing of interest to her. Nothing that rated closer inspection. As the water came to a boil, she sighed softly and resumed humming.

As I watched her, surreptitiously, the full measure of what had occurred, of what I'd done, came into ever more stark focus. That I had cuckolded Zezel was the least of it. He wouldn't mind, not under the circumstances. Given Allison Molho, I was persuaded he would not mind. But I had laid Mrs. Zezel. Laid her like tile, I thought: Like kitchen tile, I had laid her. Her nakedness now seemed to me like the face of Medusa. Not that she was less than pretty, ballerina-slim and pretty, but the sight of her turned my heart to stone. I recalled the time a year before when, accidentally, I had glimpsed her nipple as she and Zezel danced. It was at a book party for one of Zezel's academic cronies, and the music was sixties archaic. Zezel was doing his Zezel dance, an awkward shuffle step with his arms fixed at his sides, when of a sudden he grabbed his wife by the waist and began to whirl her across the dance floor. The two of them stumbled twice, almost fell, but managed to recover their balance; finally, as the song ended, he stopped in front of me and dipped her, and for an instant she spilled out of her gown. Her nipple was dark and oversized, comprising most of her small left breast. This, I did not want to know; I felt queasy with the knowledge. Now I had bitten the thing, sucked on it until her abdomen trembled beneath me, until her legs wrapped reflexively around me, until I made her moan.

Now she turned and noticed me.

"Some night, kiddo." I looked away from her, and she walked over to me. She clasped my hand and rubbed it gently across her pubic hairs, and then she pressed her cool abdomen into my side. "When we weren't doing the nasty, I kept meaning to ask you, how'd you burn that circle into the counter?"

"It was just an accident."

She arched her eyebrows. "What's the matter, baby? Blue balls?"

"No," I said. "It's not that."

"Bad conscience?"

"No." I shook my head.

"What else could it be?" She put her forefinger to her lips in mock-bewilderment. "Could it be, I wonder, that I won a round?" She slapped me on the behind and returned to the kitchen. "That's it, kiddo, isn't it? For once, I got what I wanted, and you didn't, and you don't know how to deal with it. Feeling kind of used and abused, am I right? Well, you don't have to worry. Maybe I did do this to settle the score, but I'm not going to rub his nose in it. If he finds out, it won't be from me."

"That's a comfort," I replied.

"For what it's worth," she said, "you've got it over him by a mile in the sack."

"That, I didn't want to know."

"C'mon, kiddo. You can't kid a kidder. It's what all guys want to know. How they stack up. That's the reason rams butt heads, the reason moose lock antlers. You think you're different from the rest of the herd?"

Again, I shook my head.

"Let you in on another little secret," she laughed. "Your bud's hung more like a hamster than a moose. It looks like one of those test pencils, the kind without erasers. The kind it doesn't even pay to pocket. Sometimes he does his business, and I don't even feel him going in." She slapped me on the shoulder and laughed again. "Can you just picture it? There I am, braced for a good old jackhammer, and I get stung by a mosquito. . . ."

The anger lit up my spine and arrived in my hands as rage. I caught her by the throat and spun her around to face me. She looked into my face; then, yet again, she started to laugh. The rage dissolved in an instant, and I released her.

"Not exactly your style, is it, kiddo?"

She stepped back into the kitchen and poured the coffee.

She is gone now, Mrs. Zezel. *Whether* she is going to tell her husband is not an issue. *When* she is going to tell him is the only issue. I doubt she will tell him at once. She'll no doubt want to savor the deed for a time, smile sweetly at him whenever he sneaks off to meet Allison Molho. As he leaves, she will say to herself: "He betrays me, but I have betrayed him *with his best friend.*" (I paraphrase.) The fact that Allison Molho is also Mrs. Zezel's friend, not her best friend perhaps but her friend nevertheless, is a solace for me. Mrs. Zezel did not win. She thinks she won, but she is only just ahead.

After she departed, I took a bath, a hot bath. The kind of hot bath that leaves you tan for several hours. I used strong soap on my penis—which burns even now. So it should. In the ongoing discourse between mind and genitalia, the latter understands only discipline and reward. The penal system, so to speak. Reason has no place here, or else Mrs. Zezel would never have seen the top of my kitchen counter. Thus, I took my penis between thumb and forefinger and applied strong soap to the very aperture. The sensation spread in alternate surges, warm and very hot, and lit through my entire lower guts. I believe I made myself clear.

DECEMBER 12:

After a week, here is what I have concluded: I have not betrayed Holly Servant. Love is not betrayed by the likes of Mrs. Zezel. Not in this case at least. What of the fact that I took her into my arms? That I inhaled the scent of her hair, that I parted my lips as we kissed, that I unfastened her blouse, that I feinted towards the slopes of her breasts? Love concerns itself with none of these things. As long as certain words remain unspoken, as long as certain emotions remain unpricked, the gestures hold no significance beyond a parenthetical citation. Yes, gentlemen, I lifted her onto the kitchen counter, and, yes, I deposited that which is mine, that which is most palpably of me, that which is essential, within her, and yes, afterwards, even afterwards, when she kicked open the refrigerator, I noticed the soft glow of her cheek in the refrigerator light. How could I not? But what of it? Love is not transmitted by coitus. No, not in either direction. Lovers, therefore, cannot be betrayed below the waist. The anointing is not in the oil.

But the recollection strangles me.

DECEMBER 16:

When Zezel turned up at the door this morning, I knew at once his wife had not told him yet. Perhaps she still keeps it from him because she realizes how awkward I feel. The logical move would be to tell him myself, but I won't. Not because I fear his reaction. No doubt he will be simultaneously amazed and amused—though in what proportion I cannot predict. Still, I'll not tell him myself: I would spare him the dread of a confrontation with his wife. The confrontation is inevitable, to be sure, but the dread is not. That's the worst of it. If I told him myself, Zezel is the sort to live with the dread for many weeks, to harbor the dread in the pit of his stomach until it affected his very digestion. He'd twist on the toilet for at minimum a month before he worked up the resolve to confront his wife. *That* is what I wish to spare him.

Now he stood at the door, oblivious, and said, "'Tis the season."

"Merrily, yes, but 'tis not *our* season."

"Merrily, verily, a race out of season."

"Fish out of water."

"Red herrings caught in the tuna net."

Then I thought of his hamster balls and closed my eyes. He walked past me into the kitchen, pulled open the refrigerator and took out a carton of orange juice. He stood in front of the same counter on which I had screwed his wife a week and a half before, and their two images were juxtaposed in my mind, and for an instant both Zezel and Mrs. Zezel were in the kitchen, and he took down a glass from the cupboard and set it on her bare abdomen, and he poured a glass of orange juice into it, and then I said, "Pour me a glass too."

He did, and he handed it to me.

"The burn on the kitchen counter—a Satanic ritual?"

"No, it was an accident."

"More's the pity," he said. Then he grinned. "Ever done it on a kitchen table?"

"Done what?"

He rocked back and forth with his pelvis.

"No, not on a kitchen table," I answered.

"Allison Molho and I did last week," he said, giddily. "When I came, I knocked her cappuccino maker onto the floor. Do you know what she said? The thing crashed to the floor like a thunderclap, and Daphne held me inside of her and whispered: *C'est la vie*. Just like that. *C'est la vie, baby*. Think of it! That other woman, that not-Daphne, that *wife*, once cursed me because I clogged the toilet with a longstanding movement. The cruelty! The insensitivity! Especially when the toilet is so often my waterloo! It should have been a moment of triumph, of celebration. But she paced from one room to another, waving a metal coat hanger, muttering 'I don't believe this! I don't believe this!' Afterwards, she wouldn't sleep in the same bed with me for a month."

"Neither would I," I said.

"Next month perhaps?"

"I'll check my calendar."

"*C'est la vie, baby!*"

"If you insist," I said.

"Truly, mine is a Daphne among Daphnes!"

He noticed the cardboard carton in the corner of the room, beneath the window, and his eyes lit up. "What have we here?" He was on it in an instant, seizing it in his arms like a child struggling with a bulky toy. He shook it to hear the contents, which sounded muffled and indistinct. Then, suddenly he looked up at me and frowned. "Or do I trespass again?"

"Again?"

"Perhaps I have stumbled upon another forbidden fruit . . . like that secret journal of yours?"

"No, it's nothing like that."

He began to smile and shook the carton again. "How many guesses do I have?"

"As many as you like," I said.

"Pandora's box?"

"Less nether."

"An inflatable woman?"

"Less breathy."

"Spider monkeys?"

"They're not in season," I said. "That's a hint."

"Then it's something in season. Perhaps a half-bushel of nectarines?"

"*'Tis the season,* remember?"

"Hanukkah presents?"

"Christmas decorations."

"For the Son of Man?"

"They cheer me up," I said.

"But what of the symbolism?"

"Mistletoe is mistletoe."

"Holly is holly."

I startled. "What?"

"It's a tautology, is it not? Holly *is* holly?"

I grinned. "Yes, I suppose it is."

"Then by all means, deck the halls," he said. "For within the fortnight, I will stand beneath your mistletoe with my Daphne. On that, you have my word."

DECEMBER 20:

The Christmas tree I bought last night leans against the wall. I am about to run downstairs to Woolworths for a tree stand. Gentlemen, here is a confession: Until last night, I'd never heard of a tree stand. The man at the tree lot inquired what kind of stand I had, and I could only shrug. The tree itself cost me forty-five dollars, plus another five I bribed the fellow to help me carry it home. Now it leans against the wall behind me, tethered with coarse rope like a model in a bondage magazine. There is a broad swath of evergreen needles from the front door to where the tree rests. Yet another discovery: Christmas trees shed. Have I mentioned the smell? I awakened in the middle of the night, my eyes brimming over with tears. It is the very essence of gentile childhood, of baseball mitts and Lionel trains. I rose out of bed and held the tree to my breast—as if it were Holly Servant herself. The sweet sap clotted on my skin, and the smell with it. For the rest of the night, I stuck to the sheets.

DECEMBER 21:

othing.

DECEMBER 22:

True to his word, Zezel arrived at the door with Allison Molho in tow, and at once I was certain I'd seen her before. But where? The guppy face, the blond hair to her hips . . . *I knew her.* What's more, I detected a sudden spark of recognition in her eyes as well. We'd met previously. Zezel carried on about how his heart was swollen with love, about how the two people dearest to him in the world sat in the same room. "Abide, oh moment!" he cried. But Allison Molho and I avoided one another's eyes.

The two of them kissed beneath the mistletoe, a long open-mouthed kiss that underscored the unlikeliness of their coupling—she willowy and graceful, he squat and awkward. He ran his thick hand under her skirt for several seconds until she pushed him away. Then he grabbed me and shoved me in front of Allison Molho. He shoved us together underneath the mistletoe. I faced her, and she faced me. She had no idea who I was either. We kissed, lightly, on the lips. She did not feel familiar.

Zezel then clutched both of us to his breast. He squeezed us together as though he meant to fuse our ribcages, and he buried his face between our shoulders. Then he looked up and sighed.

"We must be on our way," he said.

"More's the alas."

The moment I closed the door behind them, however, I knew: Allison Molho was the blond woman from Room 21B4.

Allison Molho was Penelope Estes's *partner*.

"What lips these lips have kissed!" I muttered.

DECEMBER 23:

othing.

DECEMBER 24:

he has uttered my name, gentlemen, and the word is made anew. No, the *world* is made anew. What a beautiful name I have! What a beautiful world! She spoke it into the telephone, my name, and I did not answer at once. I did not recognize the sound. I glanced at the telephone, at the countertop, at the kitchen. My things. My name. Then I realized whose voice it was, and I replied with great composure into the trembling phone: "Hello, Holly."

Her commercial is finished, "wrapped" was the word she used, and she is going to meet me tonight at eight o'clock at Rockefeller Center. She is going to meet me above the ice rink, and we are going to skate until ten. That is our plan. The fact that I can skate is a coincidence. When she mentioned that she'd always wanted to skate at Rockefeller Center, the die was cast. She giggled like a schoolgirl; she was not accustomed to having her way. She was nervous, she said. What did I look like? I did not tell her; I told her that I'd find her. I'd come up to her and speak a secret phrase, a phrase that only the two of us would know, and then she would know who I was: "*I don't want to wake up*" was the phrase I chose.

"It's so beautiful!" she sighed. "It's so perfect!"

"Then, afterwards—"

"The carriage ride?"

I said, "Did you think I'd forgotten?"

But I am, in fact, a good skater. When we were children, Zezel and I used to ride two trains to skate at the ice rink in Flushing Meadow Park. There were rinks nearer our homes, but we sought out the less crowded venue. Zezel required it. He was never much of an athlete, as I mentioned earlier, though he always tried hard. Even now, as a man, when he runs to catch an elevator, he gnashes his teeth and flails his arms. He has never looked graceful, not for a single moment, in the many years I've known him. Not even as he walks down the street. His spine has had a slight curvature since boyhood, but that does not account for his awkwardness—which is *of him,* substantial rather than accidental. It is as though God lost the recipe for human beings an instant before Zezel was born, faked it from memory, missed slightly, then got it back; as a result, Zezel is at war with the physical universe, at war with his own physique, at war now with his wife.

As for me, I am just the reverse. Whatever comes hard to Zezel comes easily to me. No doubt, this has bothered him over the years, but to his credit he has never allowed it to affect our friendship. The fact that I could glide backwards that first time we stepped onto the ice must have eaten at him. But he gave no hint. He only clung to the wooden guardrail and waved as I whizzed by.

Enough nostalgia: Holly Servant awaits.

DOPPELGANGED: A LOVE STORY

by Mark Goldblatt

He was urbane. He was erudite. And he was thoughtful, in the literal sense. He could discuss Onan without a blush. He could discuss Byron and distinguish obscure red wines. Tenure track from the get-go, he was goddam seminal in his field, but he is of no special interest save to remark that Guy Gunther once stabbed him in the hand with a salad fork because he hated them sissy boys.

Guy Gunther indeed is of no special interest save that, for some unknown and perhaps unknowable reason, he is after me.

And I, if I may speak openly, am especially interesting.

But I am no sissy boy. For a long time, it has been my dream to become the first one-legged hockey player to skate in the Stanley Cup Finals. Two obstacles remain in my path: 1) I have both of my legs; 2) My stickhandling leaves something to be desired. Nevertheless, I am resolved. It's like Guy Gunther used to tell me before our falling out: "You're nothing in this world unless you're first. Second is chicken shit. Look at Buzz Aldrin. Look at the Chrysler Building."[1]

He might as well have mentioned Kohoutek—which served me at the time far more than it served the astronomers. To wit: "We're going to die," she said. "The comet, the planets, even the phases of the moon are unequivocal in this regard." Thus, we joined. She with the intensity of doom, and I because I am me, and because I like to relate to women in a full and open manner. The warm tides of the Sargasso engulfed me, those dying generations lost amid the mackerel-crowded C. Ever it was: Her expression distracted, her hair gyred by the wind, her face framed against the constellations, she was fixed upon me, fixed beyond me. She was fixed, and then at last she broke. Her very ponderousness heaped out of my hands. She panted. She moaned. She cooed and bayed: Her mind moved upon silence. As the sun came over the horizon, we fell apart. She smiled and whispered, "Guy Gunther sends his love."

---

[1] At the time, the Chrysler Building trailed only the Empire State Building in terms of height.

She bared her teeth.

Guy Gunther! Guy Gunther! Why must you torment me? You flung my bullfrog against a hot brick wall, and I said not a word. You hammer-threw my goose into a tombstone; the purple guts splashed across the name, the dates, everywhere. You killed all my animals, and still I loved you like a brother. You bastard! You sadist! You fuck!

Mon frère.

So after that I was more careful. Kohoutek had fizzled, but what mattered was still intact. Summer was i-cumen in, the moist heat settling on my skin like maple syrup. Come June, I ate a power lifter. She was a flyweight and could press ten pounds more than our combined mass. Her thighs were as hard as tire rubber, clamped vice-like about my temples. She reclined upon the weight bench, her reps at the burn, and I, knees planted, her diligent spot. Our lips met. She tasted of underneath. Sweat ran in rivulets down her rippled stomach and converged to a single stream at the delta. From here, I imbibed as well. But she was all sinew, no substance. She held that Jacques Maritain had added nothing to the basic wisdom of Scholasticism. Her reading of Hooker's *Ecclesiastical Polity* was equally cursory. I wanted out.

She said, "What's wong wif my wittle huggy-poo?"

"I don't know," I replied. "It's just not working for me anymore."

"But why?"

"How can I answer that? It's everything. And it's nothing in particular."

"Hegelian!" she cried.

"You needn't resort to name-calling."

So she resorted to violence. But I was too fast for her. She threw looping roundhouse rights that had no chance to connect. Even her jabs, she telegraphed; she dropped her shoulder, and I ducked her from one end of the gym to the other. Exhausted, she collapsed beside the pommel horse. After a mandatory eight count, she began to weep.

"I'm sorry," I said.

"Sure," she sobbed. "It's so simple for you. You don't have to spend six hours a day with dumbbells. You get to go out, meet people. I never meet anybody."

"Then why keep at it?"

"Sometimes I wonder . . ."

She threw in the towel the following morning. She got soft, and then she got pregnant, after she got raped, and then one morning she was gone. Such is the *sic transit* of our inglorious *mundus*. We gather our memories about us, sift through them for lessons, an eye ever towards that Final Judgment, those Scales and Balances, that Twice-Checked List. Then something like Kohoutek happens along, and we panic. We're not ready yet! We haven't yet achieved that higher plateau! We're still unfinished, half-baked! God hasn't been square with us, creeping up like that. So to hell with it! To hell with the high road! Confident of our damnation, we desecrate, we fornicate. Kohoutek fizzles, and we repent. We sally forth to start anew.

High shticking aside, I put the sad doings of the weight room from my mind; I sallied forth to start anew. Seduction, however, has its own dialectics, and soon thereafter I scored an ice-skater. She was a sugar-plumbed fay of a girl, a whisper of pink across the cool white plane. The subtle scratch of her blades charged my senses, stiffened my strides, and the faint flowered scent of her hair trailed into my face. From one end of the rink to the other, we cut crisp eights across the ice until at last I addressed the delicate frills of her tights. She tensed against my fingertips, slowed into my embrace. "Dare we?" she inquired. But the frozen pink reluctance of her daiquiri had begun to melt. A sudden lift. She posed above me, her legs at 9:15, and I accused her through the rum-sweet soak of pink cotton. Then I set her down, and we parted for the compulsories: I tossed my sweatshirt across the ice, shredded my pants across my blades, deposited my briefs along the rail. Then I threw a couple of salchows just to keep warm. Moments later, she had stripped naked. She performed first a single, then a double lutz, her pink elfin breasts hugged under her arms. Then she dropped to a sit-spin as I drew nearer, followed by a flying camel into a double axel; for a finale, she hopped aboard the old vanguard, and we glided as one towards the end of the ice. As she sat on the rail, I gave her five-point-nine out of a possible six.

"Love," she moaned.

And I moaned, "There are other things."

So indeed there are. But often we lose sight. If love were excised from the experience of man, enough would still remain to ease his passage, to grease his slow slide back to nihil. Epistemic literature would still remain. Epistemic literature and the prehensile thumb. It might be argued, in light of these, that love is superfluous, a redundancy wrought from the overlap of the angelic and material realms. Or not. Certainly, I have loved. For instance, there was Amy.

Amy!

Amy: Once upon a time every bell chimed Amy. Every one, from the pubescent Amy of the recess bell at the grammar school down the road to the rapacious Amy of the dinner bell at the soup kitchen on the corner, every bell rang out Amy upon Amy with each wanton sway to and fro. And

I would walk the street every Sunday morning to bathe in an ocean of masses. And my doorbell was pitched to a dear lilting Amy. And my dog wore a tiny cowbell before she died. The love, of course, was unrequited. For I know nothing as deadly to love as an actual whiff of the well-beloved fish. For if a rose is a rose, and a spade is a spade, and a horse is a horse, then a fish is a fish. (Of course, of course.) If a fish were a rose, a man might bleed to death. From his tongue. So at last to ensure that my love would be pure, I pre-conceived Amy. As the Sabbath sun washed across the windows of another roach-ridden motel, I rolled off Miss Congeniality and called her "Amy."

"Who's Amy?"

"Just someone," I replied. But from the very beginning she was more, much more, than the mere flesh she lacked. For in my own image I made Amy: And when she was good, she was very good. Imagine a waterfall of tangled brown hair, a hint of fresh strawberries forever on her cheeks. And beneath that hair were high ideas, and behind those cheeks were great and gorgeous words. To come into Amy was to come into knowledge, to come into art—for the first time I felt redeemed in the act. The poetry of Keats played upon her lips. Now more than ever seemed it rich to die. And always Amy received my death, received my ashes into her dust. Yes, and if perchance I rose again, rose again from the ashes of a too sudden death, she received my resurrection with Constance and with Ardor. Neither of whom I ever bothered to invent, for the mere orifical possibilities did not interest me because I had Amy.

Still, I could not make her love me. Perform, yes. Float up and down the shaft of my penis—to be sure. But love I was unable to engender. Whatever passion I aroused in Amy never quite wrought a wound, in the way that love must wound. The anguish was absent from her eyes, utterly. And although I never asked, there was no doubt in my mind whence the difficulty. The very idea of Guy Gunther hung between us, a scrim though which only our shadows passed.

Goose-flinger!

DECEMBER 25:

No, I cannot blame Zezel for what he has done. For the fact that he has broken into my apartment, no doubt more than once, for the fact that he has broken into my journal and inserted his own material . . . for the fact that he turned up at Rockefeller Center, last night, as I awaited Holly Servant. How could I? Zezel is but an instrument of God's will, gentlemen, for He did indeed make the world, and also He made last night. Perhaps, therefore, I should begin with the Word. In the beginning was the Word, and the Word was with God, and the Word was God. Now cut to last night: For last night was made by the word, the word that became flesh, the flesh that became mine. Cut to now, to these words: These words are mine. What I once explained to Zezel, what he perhaps read with his own eyes last night, is true. These words are for me. Yes, for me, and I'll return to them for as long as I have eyes, for as long as the words have sense. For as long as the world has meaning, I'll return to these words.

So I'll begin at Rockefeller Center, where I arrived as a light snow had begun to fall. The night air was crisp, the wind like cardboard, but under my overcoat streams of sweat trickled down my back, and I shivered. As I leaned against the brass guardrail that overlooked the sunken ice rink, the Christmas tree was to my right; it was engulfed by vast throngs of tourists. The great gray monolith of the GE Building loomed behind me; I felt as though it were peering over my shoulder, leaning forward for a glimpse of Holly Servant. But she was nowhere to be seen. Again and again, I glanced at my watch, but the time never registered. So I fell to deductive logic: I had left home at six o'clock, two hours early, for the ten minute walk to Rockefeller Center; I had walked at a slow pace, stopped to eat a pretzel, then stopped to drink a soda. . . .

I was at least an hour early.

For a long time, I cannot tell how long, I stared down at the rink, at the clusters of skaters who followed the circumference of the ice surface. Several couples held hands, or locked arms for support, and there were young children clinging to their parents' coat hems. Mostly, though, it was difficult to discern who was with whom. Just clusters of people. Their breaths were streamers of smoke. Off to the side of the ice, a brass band played for them. Their instruments glistened with the falling street-lit snow, especially the tubas in the rear. Nine pieces in all. Like nine toys. The music was soft and waltzy, barely noticeable from where I stood.

"What a lovely evening!"

I spun around in horror.

Zezel was grinning at me.

"But how—?"

"I am he as you are he as you are me—and we are all *et cetera.*"

"You read my journal!"

"*Your* journal?"

"You broke into my apartment!"

He shook his head. "You gave me a key. You told me of a journal. It is I who am the victim. I was entrapped—entrapped, I say! But I forgive you." He threw his arms around my shoulders and kissed me on the right cheek. "I forgive you the totality of your trespasses."

Then I realized: He had read about his wife; he had read about Allison Molho.

"I'm sorry," I muttered.

He waved off the apology. "Water under the bridge. For now I await an angel."

Then I realized: He intended to meet Holly Servant . . . *he intended to be me.*

"Don't do this," I said.

"How can I not?"

It was a difficult question.

"Please," I said.

"What would you do if the shoe was on the other foot?"

Another difficult question.

Then I realized: "Limp!"

He threw his arms around me again, and he kissed me on the left cheek.

Now I looked him straight in the eyes. "Please."

His eyes narrowed in on mine. "The words. I need the words."

"Please . . ."

"The three words!"

Then I felt tears, single tears, rolling down both of my cheeks: "It's my heart."

Zezel smiled at me, a strangely distant, self-satisfied smile. There was a sudden gust of wind, and I closed my eyes. When I opened them again, seconds later, he had withdrawn, evaporated into the backwash of the crowd.

I brushed the tears from my cheeks and resumed my watch. Every ten minutes or so, I glanced behind me for Zezel, but after several such glances I exhaled and trusted that he was indeed gone. It was the recollection of his smile that reassured me, of the satisfaction of his smile after he'd made me utter the words. So I tried to put him out of my mind, to focus on the reason I'd come to Rockefeller Center. The reason I'd begun the journal Zezel had read. The reason I had been born: Holly Servant. Now, though, I started to worry. The encounter with Zezel had brought me down to earth long enough to tell time. So I knew that she was fifteen minutes late. Perhaps she had come to her senses, or perhaps she had been warned off by that damnable agent of hers.

I said to myself: *I don't want to wake up.*

"It's so beautiful. . . ."

I knew the voice in an instant. "Yes, it is."

I turned around.

She smiled at me, her angel face radiant through the streetlight and snow. It was a polite smile, nothing more. She had no idea who I was.

"I know you," I said.

She looked down and blushed slightly.

"From television," I said. "I know you from television."

"That was a while ago," she replied.

"But before television," I said to her, "I knew you from the heroic achievements of art, from the swells of classical symphonies and the closing pages of Russian novels. I knew you before I was born, in the dreams that opened out into a life. *I don't want to wake up.*"

Then she spoke my name, as she had spoken my name over the telephone, and I felt her breath against my face. Her breath was warm and sweet, scented with spearmint. I nodded, and her eyes brightened.

She was pleased.

As we descended the wide concrete stairs towards the ice rink, how shall I describe what was in my chest? Euphoria, to be sure. But also strangeness. Newness as well, as though the very wind of Creation swelled in my lungs. So, too, there was nausea, the kind of nausea that distances you from reality, that catches in the back of your throat as you would swallow. Several steps from the bottom, she reached out and took my arm in hers. How shall I describe what I felt just then? The warmth of her shoulder against mine, her weight angled into me. Had I stepped away, she would have fallen. She trusts me, I thought. She trusts me with life and limb on steep concrete stairs. Even now, perhaps, she trusts me enough to kiss her. But she trusts me not to kiss her until the moment is right. She trusts me not to force the moment.

"How was the commercial?" I asked.

"Please, let's not talk about that."

"We don't have to talk at all."

"No, maybe we should talk about it," she said. "My therapist tells me that I keep too much to myself, that I bottle up my feelings inside instead of letting them go. But sometimes . . . I don't know. It was for laundry detergent, the commercial, and I had to climb inside one of those great big washers, the kind where the clothes spin around and around. That was the joke. The idea was for me to wear this stained white bikini, which was supposed to come out clean at the end."

"Did it?"

"Not the first time."

"How long were you in the machine?"

"Thank God, just until it started to spin," she said. "After it filled up with water, I'd climb out, and the bikini would go through the rest of the cycle by itself. But it didn't come clean in cold water, or even in warm. So in the end I got scalded with hot. I've got like a sunburn on my tummy and thighs, and my back still hurts from getting scrunched up all afternoon."

I shook my head, but I said nothing.

"But that isn't the worst," she continued. "The worst is the stage hands, the way they look at you. It's like, there you are, dripping wet, trying to do the best job you can, and all they want is to get an eyeful. The way they look at you, they make you feel so dirty. . . ." Her voice choked off, and she squeezed my hand.

"Mr. Finkleman arranged this?"

"Let's not talk about it," she said.

We came to the edge of the ice, hand in hand, and for the next several minutes stood against the rail and stared out across the crowded glistening surface. The brass music and the hiss of skates filled our ears. She did not speak, and I did not speak. I would have been content to stand there, the two of us, against the rail, the entire night; I would have been content to hold her hand and to taste the falling snow on my tongue. The evening was bathed in soft yellow light, diffused from four beacons which shone onto the ice. The tree loomed just above us now, illuminated from its base by another two beacons. When I peeked at Holly, her gaze was fixed on the tree. Two perfect streams of tears, as pure as mine had been corrupt, glittered down her cheeks. She squeezed my hand even tighter. The band came to an abrupt halt, and I muttered, "Let's go rent skates."

The line for skates was short, five minutes, before a white-haired man handed us two pairs of ragged leather high-tops. Hers were white, mine black. The blades of both were dotted with rust, but the worn leather slipped easily onto our feet. After we laced up, she pressed a twenty dollar bill into my hand. This, I refused doggedly.

She said, "But skating was my idea."

"But New York is my town," I said, though the words sounded absurd as I formed them.

Then, as we moved out onto the ice, we joined hands again. The first steps were wobbly for her, and I rejoiced once more at her need of me. I'd felt a certain apprehension over those first several steps, an apprehension that she would glide like a ghost across the ice, that she would pirouette and twirl, that she would mention, *oh by the way,* that she'd once skated in the Olympic Trials. That she would cause a commotion by her grace and then be lost to me among a crowd of admirers. But she was a beginner. She let go of the rail only after she detected that I could skate, that I could support her.

After a couple of tentative laps, she laughed and said, "I should be much better at this. My dad used to take us skating when I was a little girl back in Winona. That's where I grew up. It's in Canada . . . near Hamilton." She laughed. "Near Toronto."

"I thought you were from Los Angeles."

"No, I've only been in L.A. for four years—since I was eighteen."

"That's very young to be on your own," I said.

"That's just what my dad said. He thought I'd end up a prostitute or something, or doing x-rated movies. That was what he thought Hollywood was like. I think it still kind of scares him a little. Actually, he's not much for the States. Just because he got mugged once in Buffalo. So do you know what I always say to him? It's *Holly*wood. Get it? *Holly*-wood. It's got my name in it."

"You're still close to him?"

"My mom died when I was seven," she said. "My dad's all I've got."

"What about brothers and sisters?"

"I had an older sister, but she killed herself when I was fourteen."

"Why did she kill herself?"

"I don't know."

"How did she do it?" I asked. "Did she hang herself?"

"No, she took pills."

"Maybe it was an accident."

"She left a note," Holly said.

"Well, then, that's that."

She smiled at me again. "You talk like a writer. You ask questions people are afraid to ask."

"Should I apologize?"

"No, people should say whatever's on their minds."

"That, I don't agree with."

"Why not?"

"Words need to be weighed before they're spoken." I stopped skating, and we slowed to a gradual halt; then I turned to face her. "What if I told you the words inside me at this very moment, if I told you of the exquisite joy of your hand in mine? If I used up those words now, what words would be left when I kiss you good night?"

She blushed at this. "You're so different from the men I know. I don't know if I've ever met a man like you."

"I have a friend like me," I said. "We're a dime a dozen."

That remark ended our conversation for the next several minutes. She was steadier on her skates now, and twice I released her hand in case she wanted to solo for a lap. But she wouldn't let go. We never lost contact, not for a second, as we coursed around and around the ice rink.

"What about you?" she finally asked.

"How do you mean?"

"Are you close with your parents?"

"They're both dead," I answered.

"How long?"

"My mother died . . . she died when I was born. My father died when I was in college."

"What did he die of?"

"Being old," I replied. "He was much older than my mother."

"They must have been so much in love—I mean, if age didn't matter."

"I don't know if age mattered," I said. "The fact that he was her English professor didn't seem to matter. So I guess if you can look past one, you can look past both."

"You probably had a lot of books around the house when you were growing up."

"Too many."

She shook her head. "You can never have too many books. I *love* books. I think books are the best things in the world. I used to get Dr. Seuss books when I was in first grade. That's how I remember my mom. Sitting with me at night and reading *Green Eggs and Ham*. I still love that book."

I brushed her cheek with the back of my hand, and she turned to face me.

Then I said, "Would you, could you, on the ice?"

She laughed loudly. "I would not, could not, on the ice."

"Holly, I'm not Sam-I-Am."

She said nothing in response. The light snow continued to fall, and I could feel it starting to stick in my hair and eyebrows. My face was warm and red with a thin film of perspiration. Out of the corner of my eye, I saw that her face had reddened as well, a glowing Christmas red. Her woolen sweater was striped with pink and white, her pants were white, and her leg-warmers were pink. She was tinted like a Christmas ornament.

Wordlessly, now, she tugged at my heart.

The snow had slowed to a veil of dust, as much updraft as fall, as we strolled up Sixth Avenue in the direction of Central Park. She had let go of my hand only to remove her skates, had taken it again as soon as we passed Radio City Music Hall, and so on we walked. The flesh of her palm in mine seemed to smolder, the warmth and heft of a new-picked peach. Now and then, she would crane her neck to take in the height of a skyscraper, the top floors shining with moonlight; the snow seemed to glitter against the dark outlines.

She said, "It must be so exciting to live here."

"You mean the buildings?"

"Not just them. Just the way it feels to walk down the street."

There was a phalanx of limousines and yellow taxis stopped at a red light at Fifty-Fifth Street. The sight of them, perhaps a dozen cars in three uneven rows, caught her eye. I watched her watching them as the red DON'T WALK signal started to flash. We paused at the corner.

"Watch what happens when the light turns green," I said.

"Even I know that—they're going to go."

"They don't just *go*," I said. "They *pounce*. They pounce on the moment."

The DON'T WALK signal continued to flash for several seconds; then the letters froze, and she inhaled deeply. The tension passed from her hand to mine. The sudden click to green: In an instant, in scattered unison, the cars lurched forward. She flung her arms around my neck.

"I felt it," she cried. "It was like they pounced on me."

She hugged me hard, and slowly I closed my eyes.

The sweet acid fumes of horse manure burned our eyes as we approached the line of carriages on Fifty-Ninth Street. There were eight of them at the edge of the park, the drivers in top hats for Christmas Eve. We climbed into the second buggy, her choice, and a moment later we were in motion. The quaint clip-clop of hooves against pavement of the street filled the air. The sound was a fine anachronism, loaded with unresolve. Holly and I huddled together in the back seat. I wondered what thoughts were in her head. Did she too hear the anachronism in the clip-clop? Did she sense the incongruity of the two of us, of *Holly Servant* and *me*, huddled together, on Christmas Eve, in a horse drawn carriage? *What's wrong with this picture?* The fact, perhaps, that the carriage drivers had an infamous record of animal abuse? That the pavement wore on the horses' brittle femurs until the bones splintered? That local humane societies had pushed for legislation to have them banned from city streets? Or was she altogether caught up in the moment? How I wanted to be caught up in the moment! But I was self-conscious, so self-conscious that I could no longer feel her shoulder against mine, the strands of her blond hair against my neck. *Watch how the cars pounce on the moment,* I thought: How often had I rehearsed that metaphor in my mind? Often enough that the words themselves meant nothing to me. She was *supposed* to embrace me afterwards . . . and so she had. I hadn't even returned her embrace. No, I'd stood with my arms dangling and thought: *The words worked.*

But that was the trouble. She'd run me the lines I had anticipated, and the evening had acquired the feel of a play—a play in which I had become a kind of actor-critic, more and more removed from the joy of performance. As we rode in the carriage, I thought: Here, then, is the distance that divides art and life, the distance that renders every work of art a failure. At best, a noble failure. At worst, masturbation. In my case, a bit of both. I felt her exhale and caught sight of her breath as she sat beside me. Yet it was not me she sat beside. I was not there. Who, then? To have come so far, to have succeeded so implausibly, and still, in the end, to fail! As I gathered my thoughts in the back of the carriage, desperation welled up inside of me.

"Stop!" I shouted. "Pull over to the side!"

The driver steered the horse towards the curb.

"What's wrong?" Holly asked.

"Take her wherever she wants to go," I said, handing the driver a fifty dollar bill. Then I hopped out of the carriage onto the sidewalk.

Holly cried out, "What did I do?"

She was half out of the carriage herself, but I caught her and prevented her from climbing down. She struggled for a second, hung onto the collar of my sweater, but then she settled back into the seat. There were tears streaming from her eyes.

"It's not you, Holly," I said. "It's me. I don't belong here. I'm not the kind of person you should be with. Not on a night like this. It's too beautiful, too perfect, too *Christmas*. The sky is too moonlit. The snow is too white. The driver is too quiet. And the horse is too . . . oh, I don't know. Too constant. Yes, that's it. The horse is too constant. He plods on and on and questions nothing. Look at him, and then look at me—"

"But you're beautiful," she said.

"Look inside of me," I said. "Look past tonight, past the postcard of the two of us, together, as the snow falls around us, as the carriage rolls down the street. Do you know who I am? Do you know *what* I am?"

"I don't care," she sobbed.

There was a tremble in her voice, a palpable ache, that made my heart hurt.

The driver grunted; he wanted to move.

I shook my head. "Holly, you don't know me."

"I don't care!"

I lifted her down onto the sidewalk.

As soon as he felt her weight out of the carriage, the driver set the horse back in motion. The carriage jerked away from the curb, a clatter of wheels and hooves, and we watched it drift out into the flow of traffic. Now we stood at the corner of Fifty-First and Fifth Avenue, across from Saint Patrick's Cathedral. We turned towards one another. Then, at once, she buried her face in my chest and wept. How her tears burned into me! But they also recalled the night Mrs. Zezel came to my door, the night she cried on my sleeve and wound up on my countertop; I struggled to put the image from my mind. How different Holly's tears were, how like the tears of a child! Angel tears, I thought, as I stared up at the stone angels of Saint Patrick's. No wonder her tears burned into my heart!

"Please don't leave me," she muttered.

I realized, at that moment, I couldn't. We remained on the corner for several minutes, an island of huddled incongruity that momentarily parted the river of pedestrians. Couples glanced at us and smiled, thinking we were kissing. Then, finally, I whispered to her, "We'd better walk somewhere."

She stepped back and clasped my hand again, and I led her north towards Fifty-Seventh Street—which I knew would be even more crowded. That was what I wanted. Crowds and crowd noises. To distract me from my thoughts. To keep me from the scripts I had concocted, half-aware, since the first letter I ever wrote to her. It was true enough; I had met her in every season. In my mind's spring, we had rowed across the lake in Central Park. Summer, we had strolled over the Brooklyn Bridge, casting pennies into the East River. Apple-picking in the Catskills was what I had imagined for the fall. Still, and always, the flaw in each scenario was the same: Me.

She spoke in a low, tentative voice as we walked. "What I said before, about you being beautiful, I just wanted you to know I meant it. Not just what you look like. But on the inside too." She squeezed my hand tighter. "If I could only get the right words to say what I feel! The way you always get the right words, if only I could get words like that! Then maybe I wouldn't need my shrink. If you've got the right words, it's like life itself is therapy."

"You don't need therapy, Holly."

"Yes, I do," she stated. "You don't know me."

"Why?"

"It's like . . . we talk about my life, my needs."

"To what end?" I asked.

"So I can understand why I do the things I do."

"But why is *that* so important? What if you just stopped thinking about it? What if you stopped trying to understand yourself and just lived? Suppose you said: *I do what I do because, at the moment I do it, I want to do it.* Wouldn't that be a saner life? Wouldn't that be a truer life?"

"I don't know—"

"Do you remember the floods in Iowa a few years ago? I was watching the news on CNN, listening to interviews with people whose entire lives got washed away. There was this one woman who was talking to a reporter, and in the background, as she was talking, her house came off its foundation and slipped past the camera. I'll never forget that. Sewers were backing up into the streets, cars were stacked on top of one another at an overpass, local kids were piling up sandbags to protect their high school. Then, suddenly, the videotape stopped. The scene shifted back to the studio in Atlanta. The anchorman introduced his special guest—a renowned psychotherapist. He asked her what emotional difficulties the victims might experience once the waters receded. The lady nodded gravely. She ran down a checklist of likely symptoms: depression, anxiety, nightmares among the children. Then she suggested that the president step in, that he appoint a psychological task force immediately. So I thought: That's just what people need when they're up to their hips in untreated sewage—a SWAT team of MSWs jumping out the back of a van and asking them to discuss their issues."

"But people need to talk about their issues."

"People with too much time on their hands," I said. "Too much time to think about themselves, about their lives. There was another report on CNN, just a couple of weeks ago, about a dying baby. I think it was in Rwanda. I watched it with a friend of mine. Do you suppose that baby's mother felt a need to talk about issues? No, she was too busy brushing the flies from her baby's forehead."

"But that's different—"

"The reason people go into therapy is because they're idle. Idle and afraid."

"But life can get scary."

"Life isn't what scares them. Death, that's what scares them. So they stop by the therapist's office once a week to remind themselves that their sins aren't sins, that their failings aren't their own fault. That no one is ever to blame for what he does, so there's no such thing as hell. That's why I pray there is one, Holly. Every night, I pray that hell exists." My voice had risen almost to a shout. I glanced over at her, and she was on the verge of tears again. "I'm sorry. I didn't mean to rant and rave. It's not therapy. It's me. If there's a hell, trust me, my bags are ticketed."

"No, what you're saying—it's true," she muttered. "I'm going to hell for the way I live."

"Not you," I said.

She shook her head. "No, it's true. My life is wrong."

"That's not true."

She stared into my face. "What hurts the most is that you think so much of me."

"But I'm a good judge of character," I said. "Trust me, Holly. Your life isn't wrong."

"I don't want to talk about it. Let's talk about something else." She glanced from side to side as we neared Fifty-Sixth Street. "What's that big black building?"

"Across the street? That's Trump Tower. There's a public restroom in the lobby if you—"

"It's beautiful!"

"Do you want to look inside? There's an indoor waterfalls."

"It's so shiny. . . ."

So we made our way across Fifth Avenue and paused before the gold-plated block letters: TRUMP TOWER. She exhaled loudly.

"Well, what do you think?"

"I didn't know it was so tall."

"It *is* a tower, Holly."

"It's like Rodeo Drive. Except it goes straight up."

There were lines to enter through the two gold-framed revolving doors centered beneath the gold-plated block letters, but off to the side was a plain glass door that no one seemed to notice; we entered through it and into the marble lobby. The glare was blinding, lights shining down from the hundred foot ceiling and reflecting, in a hundred different directions, off gold-trimmed signs and mirrored walls. There were gold-trimmed exhibit cases, lit from below, of dark clothes and leather goods, dark-uniformed men posed in front of mirrored elevators, and wave after wave of bundled tourists with flash cameras. We were carried by one such wave towards the rear of the lobby and wound up before a display of diamond rings and bracelets whose silver-embossed price tags ranged from several hundred to several thousand dollars; above the jewelry was an exhibit of glittering novelties: a sequined Coca-Cola can, a sequined pharaoh's head, and a sequined owl. The centerpiece of the collection was a jewel-encrusted replica of a Fabergé Egg.

Just then, a young Asian couple slid in beside us and stared at the egg. After a moment, the wife turned to Holly and said, "Everything in New York is so beautiful, so rich."

Holly smiled at her. "It sparkles like heaven."

People were gathering at our backs, pressing forward for a closer look, so we moved aside and walked towards the marble waterfall and the far end of the lobby. The waterfall occupied a large section of the rear wall, backlit by a dozen footlights, the water cascading from the peak of the ceiling past the lobby floor and to the lower level where it splashed into a shimmering pool.

Holly turned to me. "Do people throw in pennies?"

As I was about to shrug, a square-jawed guard who had overheard her question leaned forward and said, "No coins in the fountain, Miss."

She nodded to him, and he continued past us.

"Sorry," I said.

But as I spoke the word, she had laid hold of the hem of my coat. It was a sudden provocative gesture; her hands were very near my groin. She began to tug on the bottom button, giggling as she did, glancing up at me to discover if I would pull away or seize her hands. I did nothing. After several seconds, she had worked the button free. Then, again, she giggled. "He said no *coins.*"

She turned again towards the waterfall, closed her eyes, then let the button fall into the shimmering pool below.

"Do you want to know what I wished for?" she asked me.

I thought for a moment, then said, "No."

"I wouldn't tell even if you did. I want the wish to come true."

After Trump Tower, we stopped for a late dinner at a kosher deli—not *the* kosher deli however. As I ordered, I noticed her frowning when I asked for a side order of french fries. So I called the waitress back and substituted a baked potato.

She nodded at the change and added, "The right diet is as important as cardio-vascular exercise."

"What *is* the right diet?"

"Low in saturated fat. High in protein. Red meat is all right, but don't overdo it."

"I'll remember that," I said.

(And so I have!)

Gentlemen, she would have come home with me. Of that, I am certain. Our feet brushed together half a dozen times as we ate, and on each occasion she smiled with a knowingness that was, that *is*, unmistakable. To see that smile on her face is sufficient, I thought. Also, I was afraid. To have made love to her would have been to risk the pristine quality of the night, to play double or nothing with an unblemished memory. The stakes were too high, in other words. Safer to back off, I thought, to stash one unblemished night in the keyboard, and then to return for another day. She told me over dinner that she'd be in town until the fourth of January.

"Will I see you again before you leave?" I inquired over dessert.

She hesitated, surprised that the question had come so soon, then said, "I'd like that very much."

"Where are you staying?"

"The Hotel Beverly," she said. "Wait, I've got a card with their phone number." She fished into her gray purse for a few seconds and came out with a wrinkled business card. She laughed awkwardly. "Finky said he couldn't get me a room at the Plaza on such short notice."

I glanced at the card. "It's for women only."

"I know, I know," she said, blushing. "Maybe Finky thought he could keep me out of trouble. Is your apartment very far from here?"

"No, but it's on the West Side." I smiled at her. "Besides, it's past midnight, and I'm tired. Merry Christmas, Holly."

I kissed her lightly, sweetly, on the cheek.

"I didn't know it was so late. I've got voice-overs at nine o'clock."

"Christmas morning?"

"We never *actually* wrapped last night. I just walked out."

"Can't you be fired for that?"

She shook her head. "The video's already in the can. Without me, they'd have to re-shoot just for the voice-overs."

I glanced again at the card. "It's on Lexington Avenue, your hotel."

"Are we far from it?" she said.

"Not too far."

She said, "Then let's walk slowly."

The walk to the hotel took us almost an hour as we circled and doubled back. Then at last we stopped at the front door. Men were permitted as far as the lobby, but only under the eye of a broad-shouldered female security guard. So we paused underneath the neon sign that glowed BEVERLY, and as the snow wafted past her face, Holly embraced me. Her eyes were closed, her brow damp and glowing. I kissed her forehead, and then she raised her mouth to meet mine. But I only put my finger to her lips. Then I kissed her forehead again, and she laughed softly. "I've never met a man like you."

"So you say," I said.

"Please, call me."

"No force on earth could stop me."

Then we parted, reluctantly, and I watched as she greeted the guard behind the security desk. She waved to me one last time as she waited for the elevator, and then she . . .

He's back, the man who was following me. The man who *is* following me—again. The man who is not a policeman is back against the lamppost, back below my window, back on my tail. Broad Nose is back.

He is still there, against the lamppost. He was not, is not, a phantom of the night. That was what I prayed as I awakened. For I wrote until four in the morning, a fever of words, a blur of fingertips across the keyboard. To be sure, a kind of delirium. Still, the night is saved—once on the hard drive, and twice again on disk. Broad Nose is below the window, against the lamppost, and I am awake.

He is against the lamppost, his brown Chevy is parked across the street, and the car is ticketed. From the window, I can just make out a summons fixed beneath the left windshield wiper. He got a ticket on Christmas Eve.

He is not a cop.

As I see it, gentlemen, I have three options with respect to Broad Nose: 1) confront him on my own; 2) call Detective Lacuna; or 3) just continue with life until he makes his move. Under normal circumstances, I would choose the third option in a minute. But now there is Holly Servant to consider as well; I would not put her in harm's way. The reason not to confront him on my own is cowardice, which is a very good reason. The broad nose, the dense bushy eyebrows, the wide sneering mouth . . . their sum is violence, the gruesome crackle of a ham fist against the fine sculpted cartilage beneath my face. What I fear is neither the pain nor the after-effects but the sound. The crackle inside my ears. That is enough to rule out a direct confrontation. By process of elimination, then, I am driven to Lacuna, to the number on his card tucked safely inside my wallet. I've had no contact with him in a month and am loath to sacrifice his absence. But I see no alternative.

How I resented the sound of the dial tone, the Christmas cheer in his baritone voice! How I resent the fact that I am distracted from thoughts of Holly Servant! What the detective told me was to remain inside, to lock the door, but not to alarm the man outside. Keep an eye on him, but be casual about it. Don't linger at the window for any length of time.

"That's just common sense," I replied.

"Then do it!" Lacuna said, and hung up.

Now it is ended, the siege of Broad Nose, and there is a lesson to be learned: If you brace for a tidal wave, you often wind up getting pissed on. Lacuna arrived within fifteen minutes, plain-clothed as usual, and he approached the man as I ducked behind the window. What I anticipated was the sound of gunfire. Nothing. Not even the scuffle of shoes against the pavement. So I peered back outside. The two of them were talking, casually, familiarly, like a couple of drinking buddies. Lacuna was grinning. He placed his large black hand on Broad Nose's shoulder. The two of them walked together over to the brown Chevy, and Broad Nose collected the ticket from the windshield. Then he leaned inside the car, pulled out a billfold and handed it to Lacuna. Then the two of them walked back to Lacuna's unmarked car, parked behind the Chevy, and they climbed inside. Lacuna glanced up at my window at the last moment, before the car pulled away, but his expression said nothing.

Regardless, the man is gone.

Holly was out when I phoned her in the afternoon, after Lacuna had driven off with Broad Nose. The operator at the Hotel Beverly rang her extension thirteen times, but she did not answer. So I left a voicemail message to call me back, and the presumption, the *audacity*, sent a thrill down my spine. Here is what I thought: She *will* call me back! Six months ago, she was a flickering image on a television screen, and now I leave voice messages to which she responds.

After half an hour, she did indeed call. She was out of breath. She had been to Bloomingdale's, had been powdered and highlighted only because she asked a question about a brand of makeup. She hadn't bought a thing! Then she laughed at herself and said she must sound like a Canadian hick.

"Only a lot," I said.

She laughed again. "It's not like I grew up in the Great Northwest, next door to a moose. I was going to Toronto on my own by the time I was thirteen. Toronto is a pretty big city, you know. It's bigger than Boston."

"So is Brooklyn," I said.

"What are we going to do tonight?"

"Would you like to watch a movie?"

"Which one?"

"Not in a theater, on television," I said. "The 1954 version of *A Christmas Carol* is on tonight at eight o'clock."

"Is that the *good* one?"

"It's the one with Alistair Sim."

"That's my all time favorite," she cried. "I know it by heart. 'God bless us, everyone'—I love that movie! We can eat dinner and then go back to your apartment."

"If you feel awkward—"

"Don't be silly," she said.

DECEMBER 26:

Now I will recount what happened last night. No, that's not true. I'll recount a part of what happened last night. Many things happened that I'll not go into. For instance, a twin-engine private jet crashed in Indonesia. Six lives were lost, six souls, five passengers and the pilot. That was the first piece of news I heard this morning when I awakened to the sound of the television. Then I switched off the television and rolled over in bed. Holly kissed me, and I fell back asleep.

But I've gotten ahead of myself.

Holly suggested pizza for our Christmas dinner. She had never tasted New York pizza, but her old pal Nicole from the Sunrise Workout once told her it was the closest thing to heaven on earth. So we arranged to meet at Nat's Pizzeria around the corner from my apartment. The place was deserted. Just the two of us and a hairy-armed man behind the counter who did not want to be there.

As he shoved our two slices into the oven, Holly whispered in my ear, "Do you think that's Nat?"

I turned to the man. "Are you Nat?"

He rolled his eyes.

"No, he's not Nat," I said to her.

Not-Nat slapped the two slices onto paper plates, then tossed the plates onto an orange plastic tray. Two fruit drinks filled out our order, and Holly carried the tray back to a corner booth. I handed Not-Nat a ten dollar bill, told him to keep the change and then followed her.

How she tugged at my heart, gentlemen! The first bite that she took seared the roof of her mouth, and she grabbed for her fruit drink. She held the cup in both hands, like a child, and gulped until she was coughing and laughing at the same time. "It's not funny," she said. But she continued to laugh and to fan her mouth with her hands. Her second bite was a disaster as well, the entire skin of hot mozzarella peeling off in her teeth and plopping onto her paper plate. It lay there like molten lava. She stared at it in disbelief as I hurried back to the counter. I returned seconds later with two sets of knives and forks, and she laughed again. Then, without warning, she wrapped her legs around mine under the table and smiled. She said softly, "I like to touch you."

"Why?"

"Don't you like to be touched?"

I said, without conviction: "Yes."

"Do you think I'm too trampy?"

"That's an odd question," I said, "in light of what I wrote in the letters."

"What scares me," she muttered, lowering her eyes, "is that maybe I can't live up to the way you think of me. I want to be who you think I am. But I'm scared that maybe I can't make it, and that you'll be disappointed."

"It's not possible for you to disappoint me, Holly."

She smiled at me, a slightly coy smile, then brought her gray purse onto the table. For several seconds, she rifled through it until at last she pulled out a single folded sheet of paper. She passed it to me, still folded, over the pizza. I held it in front of me and then looked back at her. But she avoided my eyes, stared down at the food as I unfolded the paper. It was a poem:

THE BREATH OF THE NIGHT

The night breathes into me
Like a lover, whispering
In my ear. But I can't

Make out the words. Maybe
There are no words, just
The breath of the night.

"Did you write this?" I asked.

"It's not my best poem, just a silly one. But at least it's short."

"I think it's beautiful," I said—which was the truth.

"Really?"

"Holly, I wouldn't lie about your poetry."

"Because it used to be a lot longer, about twenty lines. But then I started to show it to my friends, to the girls on the Workout, to the techs and crew. Not writers, just people. Not that writers aren't people, but sometimes it's nice to get the opinion of someone who isn't a professional, you know? It's like with acting. Sometimes you get so caught up in what the critics are saying that you don't stop to hear the applause. The critics hated Sunrise, by the way. Just *hated* it. They said it was T&A. But I'd like to see one of them try and do the whole workout. What I mean is . . . we must've been doing *something* right because the ratings were always good."

"What did your friends think of the poem?"

"They liked it, I guess," she said. "Bess asked me to autograph the copy I gave her. But that's just Bess. She was like the den mother to the rest of the Sunrise girls. But the thing is, well, a lot of them had one or two lines they didn't like. Never the same ones either. So I rewrote it and rewrote it until it was down to ten lines, and then to six lines. Why, is there a line in it you don't like?"

"No, I think it's perfect."

"C'mon!"

"The images are precise and concrete. The lines have a distinctive rhythm. Even the words are musical. I don't know what I'd change." I read the poem again, aloud. "Do you hear it, the music? The words sing."

"To hear that from you," she said, "you have no idea how much that means to me."

We left the pizzeria fifteen minutes to eight, enough time for a slow stroll back to my apartment before the movie began. The sky was dark blue and cloudless, lit by a full white moon. The snow from the night before had been shoveled into six inch drifts at the curbsides, and the sidewalks were rivers of gray slush. Holly's feet seemed to skim above the wetness, her boots heeled high, her red parka billowing out like a sail. When I held her hand, I did not feel myself walk.

She hesitated as we entered the apartment, and I stood behind her, just inside the front door. Then, an instant later, she noticed the door to the bathroom and darted straight for it. The time was seconds before eight o'clock. The radiator was clanging with sporadic bursts of heat; the windows were foggy with steam. I cast off my coat and sank down onto the couch, suddenly breathless. The reality of her in my apartment, in my bathroom, urinating—I could hear her!—sucked the breath out of me. I managed to lean forward for the remote control and switch on the television. The overture to the movie sounded, and I rolled back my head. She shouted to me from the bathroom. I couldn't quite make out what she said, something about how I had trimmed the tree. I didn't have the breath to ask her to repeat herself.

"This is so cozy," she said, emerging from the bathroom. "The snow outside, the dry heat. There are no real radiators out in L.A., just central air and climate control. Back in Winona, we used to crowd around the stove on cold winter mornings. Me and Dad and Lolly—that's my sister. Her real name was Lorraine, but we called her Lolly. As in Lolly and Holly. Those were good times."

"What did you say before about the tree?"

"I said it was just how I like it. Not too many decorations. Enough so you know it's Christmas, but not so many that you can't see the tree."

"It's my first one," I said.

"Can I ask you a personal question?"

"Feel free."

"From the name . . . I kind of thought you were Jewish. Not that that matters to me. The best boyfriend I ever had was this orthodox Jewish guy I dated in high school. He was so sweet. Except we had to hide from his parents all the time. He was the first boy who ever got to third base. It was in the back room of his dad's tailor shop."

"Back in Winona?"

"Yes."

"Did he please you?"

"That's a funny question," she said, grinning. "The first time is never very good, and I think it was his first time too. Neither of us knew what we were doing. Not to mention we were both scared out of our wits that his dad would find us. It was over in about ten minutes. We got undressed, did the deed, got dressed again and locked up in ten minutes."

"Not much romance there," I said.

"What about you?"

"What about me?"

"Are you . . . you know . . ."

"A virgin?"

She roared with laughter. "No, are you Jewish?"

"Well, I'm not a virgin."

"It's okay if you don't want to answer."

"I'm Jewish," I said, "except for Christmas."

"I don't think you can go back and forth."

"Why not?"

She thought for a moment. "What about baptism?"

"Ah," I said, "the old visible sign."

"Doesn't it matter to you?"

"Not at the moment. Maybe in the future."

She began to frown.

"God knows what's in my heart, Holly. When the time is right for the visible sign, I'll sense it. Then, if my heart is right, I'll do it. I'll get baptized. Meanwhile, I reserve Christmas as a kind of free trial period."

She sighed. "Well, okay, but I'm not sure it counts unless you're baptized."

Now we settled down on the couch to watch the movie. She was caught up after the first several minutes, caught up and then drawn in, siphoned from the reality of the couch, from the reality of my apartment, siphoned into the lives of the characters on the screen; I watched her watching them, watched her cringe at Scrooge's words as if they were aimed straight at her, and I felt unwashed and unbaptized for what I'd done, for the fact that I'd summoned her into existence, for the fact that she was sitting on the couch, beside me, that she was flesh and blood sitting on the couch and not a dance of electrons on the TV screen. Her grape-wide eyes were damp, about to spill over. The first tear was a great and glistening droplet, a thing of unspeakable beauty tracing down her cheek. After it had run its course, I reached across to her and brushed it away with my thumb. She turned towards me with a sad smile. Now, at once, there were two streams of tears. She said, "What a fool I must seem like." I leaned forward and kissed her face, kissed each new tear as it welled up and over.

Then, at last, I thought: Now I am baptized.

As the movie ended, she recited the last line along with Scrooge: "God bless us, every one." Then she blinked twice, wiped away a last gush of tears, and patted the couch. "So does this open into a bed?"

"Yes," I muttered.

She stood up and I opened out the mattress, and we sat down on the very edge. Then, suddenly, she kissed me hard on the mouth, a fierce kiss. We rolled backwards with the force of it, with her on top of me. Her stomach pressed against mine, now taut and now lax, as our breaths fell in rhythm. The noises she made were child-like, from the recesses of her throat, the kind of rapturous *oooh's* and *mmm's* that are checked by adulthood, that I felt as well but couldn't loose. How that rapture ran through me! No matter that I couldn't voice it, I was a child again in her arms. A creature of the senses as I undid her blouse: I was blessed. There was ignorance once again in my fingertips, abandon in my desires. What I wanted of her body, I *had* to have. And she gave to me, freely. She wrapped herself around me a dozen different ways, a woman without bones. Beneath her arms, she smelled of childhood, of hairlessness. She *was* hairless, or just about. Even between her legs, the tufts were fine and blond, virtually invisible. There, I discovered a light dew, like a child's sweat. There I lingered, with unrecognizable words on my lips. What I pronounced into her, I have no idea.

She was not beside me when I awakened in the morning. The television was still on from the night before, and I felt for the remote control on the nightstand and switched it off. Then I felt her lips against my forehead. She stood over me, and I managed to smile at her. I ached everywhere and hurt nowhere. She leaned down and whispered in my ear, "It's early, honey. Go back to sleep."

At nine o'clock, I awakened again. The desire to remain in bed was strong, but the smell of coffee was hovering in the apartment, and I rose to it. I started to wrap the bedspread around me but gave up and walked naked into the kitchen. Holly sat in a pink leotard, her workout leotard, at the kitchen table. There was a plate with crumbs in front of her, and a coffee mug, which was drained. She did not notice me at first; she was staring down at the pages of a manuscript. Beside the coffee mug lay an open manila envelope. Across the front of the envelope, several words were printed in dark magic marker: "DOPPELGANGED: A LOVE STORY (SECOND VERSE)."

That scamp, I thought.

She looked up at me and whistled playfully.

"I don't know where my bathrobe is," I said.

"I like looking at you." She walked over to me and ran her fingertips across my chest. Then she kissed me lightly on the shoulder. "I think the human body is beautiful. It's like a work of art."

"The coffee smells good. But it's not instant."

"I bought it at the corner store," she said. "There was an old pot underneath the stove. My dad used to say that coffee isn't coffee unless it comes out of a pot. That's how come it smells so good—because you're used to instant. I also got you a low fat bran muffin. It's in the fridge."

"How did you get back inside?"

"I left the door unlocked. I was only gone five minutes." She bit my earlobe, then kissed the nape of my neck. Then she looked back over her shoulder into the kitchen. "What happened to your countertop?"

"It got burned," I said.

"It's a perfect circle."

"I set down a pan on the counter. It seared the Formica. I should have known."

She laughed. "No, I do stuff like that all the time." Now her eyes met mine, and a sheepish expression came into hers. She nodded towards the manuscript on the table. "I found it there. I didn't know you wrote stories."

"Yes," I said. "Do you like it?"

"I don't know," she replied. "It's so, well, it's just so different from the article about the Chinese man. Maybe because it's a story. It's just so . . . *weird*. But I like it. It's just not my kind of story."

"Why not?"

"No, it's none of my business."

"But I value your opinion," I said.

"It's just that . . . it seemed like you were trying to show off how smart you are."

I had no clue what she was talking about. "Maybe that was the point."

"But why?"

"So that you would think I was smart."

"Then it worked, I guess," she said. "But I still like the article you sent me better."

"That's your prerogative."

She kissed me on the shoulder again. "Don't be mad at me."

"On the contrary, I'm grateful," I said. "What you think of the manuscript means more than what I think of it. Because your judgment comes from the heart, and your heart is the dearest thing in the world to me."

She walked back to the table and sat down again in front of Zezel's story. Then, at once, she looked up at me. "What if I told you I was falling in love with you?"

"I'd beg you to reconsider."

"No," she said, "I mean it. Be honest."

"I am being honest, Holly. The reverse makes perfect sense—that I should love you. But it makes no sense whatsoever that you should love me. So, if you told me you were falling in love with me, I'd beg you to reconsider because the world *should* make sense. I prefer a world that makes sense."

She stared straight at me. "Then you *do* love me?"

"I prefer a world that makes sense."

"Do you or don't you?"

"I do. I always have. I always will."

Holly stood up, suddenly, dramatically, and rushed into my arms. I returned her embrace with reluctance at first; but in the space of several heartbeats, I surrendered—to her, to her embrace, to the moment. Then I took her by the hand and led her back to bed.

She was in the shower when Detective Lacuna called at four o'clock. His voice, even over the telephone, startled me. He was an incongruity, an intrusion of the real world on the fiction I was living out with Holly. I had become accustomed to being who and what I willed myself to be. Now he addressed me as who and what I was.

He said, "Your man's clean."

"Who is he?"

"That's privileged information."

"What does that mean?" I said.

"It means I don't owe you a damn thing, not even this phone call, but I'm making it because I don't want you looking over your shoulder. It means you weren't straight with me on the Collins case, so why should I be straight with you?"

I winced. "I should've been straight with you. I regret that now. Truthfully, I regret it. But I've already told you what I know— everything. There is nothing else. I'll swear on a stack of Bibles."

He began to smile; I could hear him smiling through the phone.

"We got our man," he said, finally.

"Aubrey Collins's killer?"

"Made the arrest last night. Got the confession this morning."

"Who did it?"

"Nobody," Lacuna said. "Just a homeless guy, a crackhead."

"Why?"

"Needed cash. Watched Collins turn a trick. Then did him."

"For money? That's it?"

"That's it," he said.

There was a pause.

"Your man's a private detective from out West. Kind of a hard-ass, but his story checked out. He's being retained by a firm called Finkleman Associates to keep an eye on you. Said you'd been harassing one of their clients, an exercise girl. Mean anything to you?"

"What did you tell him?"

"That you were harmless."

"Thank you," I said.

"Did I tell him right?"

"Yes, I'm harmless."

"Just a man with hobbies," Lacuna said, laughing.

Finky had stuck a tail on me. The rage inside me was glowing hot. The man who shoves Holly Servant out of airplanes and into washing machines had stuck a tail on me. Not only that, he'd provided Lacuna with leverage to humiliate me, to undercut the miraculous love I seemed to inspire in Holly Servant and to remind me that I was doing it with mirrors. For the first time, now, I tried to imagine Finkleman's face: thick with flesh, flat in features, with perhaps a hint of mayonnaise at the edge of his mouth. That was how I imagined him, for detestable men should look detestable, smeared with high-cholesterol condiments.

Holly emerged with a surge of steam from the bathroom and nuzzled me on the back of my neck. Her skin smelled of plain soap, not the deodorant bar I kept on the dish inside the shower. She'd used the hand soap from the sink. Her hair smelled of raspberries. She had pulled a pink towel from the linen closet and wrapped it around her. But it was too small. Her breasts were covered, but the crest of her pubic hair was exposed underneath. That was where I touched her.

"What's wrong?" she said. "Something's different."

"There was a man following us last night," I said.

"Are you sure? How do you know?"

"He's staked out my apartment off and on for a couple of months. Ever since your Mr. Finkleman hired him to spy on me."

"Finky hired him?"

"Yes."

She began to smile, slightly, hesitantly. "Well, I'm sure it's nothing personal. He's only looking out for me. We used to get a lot of strange mail on the Sunrise show. Not just me, all the girls. We got marriage proposals — but also lots of dirty stuff. Sometimes, you know, it's hard to tell the weirdoes and nut jobs from the sincere fans. I guess, after I showed him your letters, Finky just got over-protective."

"Maybe he was jealous," I snapped.

The words wounded her at once, and to the core. Her mouth

curled under, and her lower lip began to tremble. The pout alone was heartbreaking. But then came the tears, *again* I had brought her to tears, and a storm of them now came—not silently as before but with a violent rush of sobs. She dropped the towel an instant later and ran naked back into the bathroom. Then, after several seconds, I followed her, still bewildered by her response. I knocked softly on the door, and she asked me to hand in her clothes.

"What is it?" I called to her. "What's the matter?"

"Nothing, I just want to leave."

"Five minutes ago, you told me you loved me."

"Maybe I was confused."

"What's wrong? Are you sleeping with Finky?"

There was no answer.

"That's it, isn't it?" I said. "That's what you were talking about last night, the great wrong in your life, the reason you're going to a therapist."

"It's the reason I'm going to hell," she cried.

I struck the door with my fist. "Let me in, Holly."

"What's the use?"

"There's no use," I said. "There's no point. There's no significance. There's just a bathroom door, and you're on the inside, and I'm on the outside, and I'm asking you to open the bathroom door."

She opened the door and stood before me. The two of us stood at the threshold of the bathroom, both naked, and she did not look at me, and I did not know what more to say. Nothing came to me. Then, without warning, without another word, she threw her arms around me.

Gentlemen, in that instant, in that split second this very afternoon, I knew what I knew, and I knew that she loved me.

Holly left the apartment at dusk for the Hotel Beverly. She did not want to go, but Finky was in town. He had caught the red-eye from Los Angeles the night before. She'd agreed to meet with him. But she was going to confront him, she swore. She was going to tell him about us. She was going to tell him that the two of them were finished . . . as lovers at least. On that, she was resolved. If he still wanted to be her agent, fine. If not, fine.

But she was afraid, and she swayed drunkenly in my arms.

I asked her if she wanted me to come with her. But she shook her head. No, she must do this herself.

She kissed me one last time, and then she left.

For several minutes afterwards, I lay on the couch. Mentally, I was drained. The images of the evening before, the wild swings of emotion, the voice that was mine yet never quite me—the sum of it tightened around my thoughts like a leather skin. I could not husk myself out of the memories. As I lay on the couch, I recalled what Holly had said about Zezel's manuscript. I walked to the kitchen and sat down at the table where the manuscript still lay. The thought of reading appalled me. Nevertheless, I began to read:

DOPPELGANGED: A LOVE STORY

(Second Verse)

by Mark Goldblatt

Now among the reasons I count myself especially interesting is the fact that I am the world's greatest lover. And I state this without fear of contradiction, for to be contradicted is to be taken at your word— which, of course, is rare enough in this life. But as a matter of fact, I am the world's greatest lover. Moreover, I have achieved this distinction without recourse to topical ointment or implant (Yeats, I am informed, had himself injected with liquefied monkey-balls in order to prolong his manhood . . . the center could not hold.) and indeed have become the world's greatest lover despite the fact that I was once something of a *shlimazl*. The kind of guy who couldn't win for losing. Guy Gunther, for example, used to challenge me to move a glass of red wine across a lacquered coffee table by sheer mentation. Yet after I managed it, for telekinesis is in fact my particular gift, I often lost control and

sent the glass tumbling over the edge. The audience
would then start to hiss, holding mere legerdemain
to blame for the rorschached carpet. Then, too,
there was the problem that the trick only worked
sometimes. For years I tried to solve the riddle
of why my powers functioned sometimes and not
others. Why sometimes, after an hour of begging
off, I would work miracles for friends; why other
times, when the power seemed to swell inside of
me, the wine might have evaporated before the
glass budged. Then at last I struck upon the answer:
Only when I was nervous was I able to perform.
Still, this answer brought new and unanticipated
twists of anguish for me. Posed anxiously before
the wine glass, I'd feel the power come . . . and
then I would relax and feel the power subside . . .
which then made me anxious again, and the power
returned . . . and so on. Finally, I quit the thing
all together. For years, I renounced my gift and
admitted to whatever sleight of hand the skeptics
suggested. The very claim to which every wooden-
nickel psychic aspired, I renounced and cursed.

Then it happened. There was a mixer at the local
night club, and Serendipity wound up beside me at
the bar. I fumbled with a line. ("I've been staring at
you for a while, and I've come to the sad conclusion
we've never met."[2]) She steeled herself for a polite
dismissal. Her eyes searched in either direction; I
ordered her the wrong drink. ("Vodka tonic? Oh,
I thought you said Vodka Collins. Bartender . . .")
"Look," she began. Then I imagined her panties.
With desperate sadness, I imagined that which I
would never know.

"Uh," she said.

She glanced angrily down at my hands. They

---

[2] For M.L. *Il miglior shlimazl.*

rested on the bar. "But . . ." she muttered. " . . . uh, uh, uh." She glanced down at her lap, stood up to examine the barstool. Then, suddenly, she clutched her lower abdomen: "Ooooh." Her eyes rolled back in her head. Then, at last, I realized what was going on.

And I smiled.

Serendipity rolled off my bed, tongue-tied and tickled pink, the following afternoon. 'Twas love, she swore. That evening did nothing to dim her words, nor the one after that. But as more and more I came to trust her words, I began to relax *in medias res*. Relaxed, I was once more a *shlimazl*. She understood for the first few off-nights, but within a week she was as dried cut-wise as a linguistics text. Once I sensed her slipping away, of course, I tensed up and had her chewing the walls again. Then I relaxed again, and she bought a vibrator. The pattern continued for several months until at last she deserted me for good. "Consistency counts," she declared, and left to pursue other hobgoblins.

Still, there was a lesson to be had: If I were to utilize my gift to its particular advantage, lingering involvements were out of the question. For as long as the faintest anxiety could be preserved, I never failed. Screams in the night entailed a new address every month. Traces of blood ruined the collars of my best shirts. Round 'em up and move 'em out. I worked the uptown meat markets like meat markets. Polled 'em at the entrance, then herded 'em out the back door. Legends snowball like legends: My name was scrawled across the walls of a hundred ladies rooms. Back at the bar, their eyes told me that they believed. Sudden hot kisses I drank like water; I'd no time for flirtations. Eventually, I even gained a measure of control: I worried about jealous husbands and jilted lovers, about crabs and herpes, about the vagina dentata and the prospects of an Israeli-Palestinian accord, about bad knees and rink madness. Then I worried about whether I could continue to worry. Whenever these would not suffice, there was always Guy Gunther to consider. Back upstairs, images of greater gists than mine martyred a new convert against the wall. The Ontological Argument was mere foreplay—each night I reproduced the Five Ways of Thomas! The metaphysical thrust of centuries, I fixed in a single moment. Afterwards, I collected their come in Dixie Cups to pour over my waffles.

Meanwhile, I continued—still continue—to pursue my hockey ambitions. End to end, rush by rush, I hone and develop the skills of my craft. Already my slapshot is hard, if slightly erratic, and I skate fast enough to fill the wing on breakaways. Right wing, in fact, is my position. Left wing is out of the question since the left leg is the one I plan to lose. On the left wing, I would be compelled to shoot backhanded exclusively or else skate backwards from inside the point. The right wing, on the other hand, would enable me to glide along the boards until the blue line, pushing off my stick and then driving off my right leg, and finally swoop towards the net for a forehand blast. Naturally, this is mere conjecture. Whatever skills I acquire as a biped may not translate afterwards.

The discovery early on that my telekinetic powers were of no use in this arena was a bitter disappointment. The puck moved too fast for me to get a fix on, and besides I kept getting cross-checked. The last time I tried, three of my teeth got knocked out. When I came to, the dental hygienist was shaking her head side to side.

"It's part of the game," I explained.

"It's barbaric."

"Too much of the world is civilized," I said. "Elemental man is an endangered species. Social norms are imposed on us to a degree that we no longer recognize the perversity of our own longings. Yet if we deny our longings, we deny ourselves. That would be dandy—if the denial were individual. Then every denial would constitute a kind of affirmation, another rung up the ladder towards Something Greater. But now morality is legislated. Noble acts are the law of the land. But the law of the land does not guarantee anything beyond death. When the dirt hits the pine, where was the gain in collective self-denial?"

These words I spoke into her, each syllable passing one by one into the moistened mammalian envelope below her beige smock. She began to tremble. The harsh surgical light glistened off the steel probe in her hand as she strained to compose herself. Sweat beaded on her nose, and across the fine slope of her chin. Her struggle amused me; for several minutes, I eased up. She adjusted the frames of her glasses, poked and nudged the gums in the back of my mouth. "Bite down," she said. Instead, I focused on the shape of the probe. Armed with the image, I traced the hypothetical circumference of her underbrush. Her breath fell hot across my face. I reached up and removed the probe from her fingertips, pulled her onto the chair. Now I felt her tongue probe those same gums, still warm with traces of blood. She was naked beneath the smock, a mouth of drool against my lap; I worked my hand underneath her, worked my forefinger inside of her. Where I could not reach, I envisioned the long cool steel of the probe. "Spit," she begged me. She reared up, and her eyes rolled back in her head. Then she held my face to her chest, and one by one I bit off the small tan buttons of her smock. The taste of her flesh was salted and clean. Caught in the momentum, I sucked and gnawed. She had unzipped my pants, and I lifted her onto me. The rhythms of the moment were gathering between us, drawing us ever inward, ever away from each other, ever towards the final release. "Bite down," she begged me.

"Mmmnph," I said.

"Take a deep breath," Guy Gunther said.

The mask passed over my face as the room went dark.

To my astonishment, I woke up. The note taped to my chin read: *"Sorry, old pal. Couldn't afford the malpractice insurance."* So that is how I was saved by the Jews. Nevertheless, I resolved to put distance between myself and Guy Gunther, to counter his ubiquity with my scarcity. But where to go? Opportunity knocked in the person of the Spiderwoman, whom I encountered at a university gala for the underclass. She was sipping cognac when I noticed her; booted in crocodile, fingernailed to the nines, she stared straight at my fly. I led with a formulated phrase: "Arach, my love, you do me long."

She raised her eyebrows. "Parlor games?"

Together, then, we undertook the dark continent. As the 747 started its final descent to Kinshasa, she got giddy and began to talk rhetorical strategies: "It's all in denial," she stated. "Whenever confronted with a rational argument, three phases of denial are in order. First, you deny the bona fides of your opponent. Refer to him as 'a mouthpiece for the dominant discourse community.' Rant at him. Put him on the defensive. If that doesn't work, you deny the body of his evidence. Refer to it as 'the propaganda of the status quo.' That should vex him good. But if all else fails, you can still deny logic itself. Point out that logic has always served as 'a tool of Eurocentric subjugation,' or perhaps 'the last refuge of the colonial enterprise.' Do you see the beauty of it? The only way your opponent can respond is with more logic—thus, underscoring your point. Your position becomes invincible!"

"What about common sense?" I ventured.

"Common sense!" the Spiderwoman huffed. "Common sense is responsible for oppression in the first place! Common sense tells us that things generally have only one meaning, that the world is pretty much as we perceive it, and our way of perceiving it is the natural self-evident one. We know the sun goes round the earth because we can see that it does. At different times common sense has dictated burning witches, hanging sheep-stealers and avoiding Jews for fear of fatal infection."

"Wow," I said. "You're good."

She blushed. "Well, I borrowed that particular passage from a literary theorist,[3] but you get the idea."

The plane touched down, and my ears popped. Then I saw the Congo, creeping through the black. Back in the hotel, it was a boomlay, boomlay, boomlay, etc. But she would not be satisfied, so we lit out the following morning. The brush was as dense as a UNLV crib-note, as dank as morning mouth. The sun scorched. Deeper and deeper, we pursued her roots. We sought shelter down river

---

3 See Terry Eagleton's *Literary Theory* (Minneapolis: University of Minnesota Press, 1983), p.108.

among a stretched-lip tribe who claimed never to have heard of the NAACP. But I was suspicious; they wore sansabelt slacks and mumbled under their breath about the bias of standardized tests and the lack of self-esteem among their children. That night, after a feast in our honor, the elders of the tribe parted to reveal the singular figure of a white man. As the Spiderwoman and I stepped forward, the stranger's face came into view. It was my face. He stood on one leg and a crude wooden crutch, and he grinned at the two of us—the Spiderwoman and myself. Save for the lack of a second leg, he was a dead perfect doppelganger. It was eerie. He introduced himself in my own voice; he spoke my own name. He spoke my own name in my own voice. Then he glanced down at the stump below his left knee and said: "I meant to do that."

For a time, the two of us co-existed. But eventually his presence grew tiresome. Wherever I turned, I found that I was already there. Worse still, when we gathered around the fire every night, he and I, the Spiderwoman and the rest of the tribe, he would regale us with stories from my life. The liberties he took! So at last I confronted him. What made him think that he was me? He scoffed at the question and said that he had been me for his entire life, except for those six months in which he had been us, but the doctors had given him special pills and now he felt much better. Since he had a long history of being me, he argued, and since he had lived that long history through to this very moment, he had every reason to suspect that he was still me—notwithstanding the evidence before his face.

His logic upset me in the extreme.

But at last I struck upon a clear solution.

When I shook the bottle, however, it grew murky. Turned out to be chocolate drink. As it happened, a trial six-pack of the stuff had been dropped from a helicopter, by a market analyst, along with several paper straws and a half-dozen rubber nipples. But I sneaked a bottle for myself and rested on a hollow log. Mosquitoes buzzed around my face. Chocolate coated the back of my throat.

Then, at last, I came up with a way out.

"Eureka!" I cried.

The chocolate muffled my voice.

That very night, over dinner, I challenged the imposter to prove that he was indeed me . . . by telekinesis. So I dared him, "Move that cup of human blood."

He regarded the cup with disdain.

"Well?" I demanded.

"It's too simple," he responded.

"Too simple?"

"It doesn't work if I'm relaxed." He looked me dead in the eye. "Why don't you try it?"

But then I realized, with a sudden rush of horror, that I'd grown overconfident in the success of my gambit. That, like the imposter, I too had relaxed—and therefore had lost control over my psychic abilities.

At that exact moment, the cup began to inch across the table.

"There!" he and I cried in unison.

The Spiderwoman threw up her arms.

"Look," I said to him, "if you're me, then why are you here?"

"Where else would I be?" he asked.

"If I were you," I answered, "I know I wouldn't be here."

He grinned slyly. "Then why are you?"

"He is with me," the Spiderwoman stated.

"Are you certain?" the imposter asked, even more slyly.

She glanced back and forth at the two of us, nervously.

That night I slept alone. The Spiderwoman crawled to the far end of our hut and curled up in a fetal position. She made a lame menstrual excuse, but after midnight I watched her tiptoe off to the imposter's hut. "The last straw," I muttered under my breath. Then I felt for it in my back pocket. But when I crept out to check, all six bottles of chocolate drink were empty.

Regardless, just after daybreak, I accosted the imposter on his morning limp. We wrestled awkwardly, and for a long time, in the course of which he wounded my hip, but in the end I pinned him to the damp jungle floor. He confessed all. He'd come to Africa, he sobbed, to forget. To forget a woman. He wouldn't speak her name. But he had loved her at the perfect moment of her beauty, and she had broken his heart. So he turned to fiction. He became a novelist in order to make women do whatever he wanted—at least on paper. He wrote like a fiend, churned out a half dozen traditional manuscripts, but in the end he abandoned realism for high shticking. No more characters, no more plot, just cut to the chase: Sex and violence and gratuitous cosmology. Then, as the book climbed the bestseller lists, he fled to Africa in a spasm of misanthropy.

"Why Africa?" I asked.

"I tried Latin America," he said, "but I was hailed there as a genius."

So I let him up.

He brushed the grime from his loin cloth, and I fetched his crutch. He smiled warmly at me. The expression on his face was less mine at that moment, though I did not recognize whose expression it resembled. Still, it was a dewy-eyed and gentle expression, a likable expression.

I said, "You're not me after all."

"If I were you," he laughed, "Guy Gunther would be after me."

The words were no sooner spoken than Guy Gunther jumped up from behind a clump of bushes and cried, "Die, dog!" He opened fire in my direction. Cat-quick from the many years of his pursuit, I hurled myself behind a large rock. The stream of his ammo ricocheted in every direction, a hubbub of bright yellow sparks, and seven or eight rounds caught the imposter flush in the chest. He fell in a heap beside me as Guy Gunther receded once again into the bush.

Now I knelt down and cradled the imposter in my arms. He struggled to speak, but only spit-bubbles came from his mouth. His eyes began to search. His gaze fixed alternately on the sky and on my face. He reacted to both in the same way, with a vague smile. But then he drew solemn. He gathered himself with his last breaths, shut his eyes, and then he named her. He spoke her name lovingly, as if to summon her into existence. These, I assumed, were his last words, so I set him down. But before I was able to stand up, he clutched me by the shirt sleeve and whispered: "Carry on for me."

As if I hadn't been carrying on already!

When I came to the end of Zezel's manuscript, I set it down on the kitchen table and thought: *That scamp!*

DECEMBER 27:

usk. No word from Holly, no word since yesterday, since she left my apartment to meet with Finky, and she has not returned the phone messages I've left for her at the Hotel

Beverly. Cause for concern, no doubt. For either she has decided to ignore my calls, my seven calls, or else she is no longer at the hotel. Either way, a drastic change has occurred. I should never have allowed her to confront Finky on her own. He wasn't beyond using his fists on her. Of that, I was convinced. His mayonnaise-greasy agent fists. I should have gone with her.

Something very bad has happened.

If the telephone doesn't ring in the next hour, I am going to walk over to the hotel myself.

DECEMBER 28:

She is gone, gentlemen. She has checked out of the Hotel Beverly, and she did not leave a forwarding address. It was no mistake either, no oversight. The desk clerk humored me; he checked and cross-checked the computer's records as beads of sweat trickled down my back. Then, at once, I glanced behind me. The broad-shouldered female guard was shaking her head from side to side.

As I walked from the lobby, I felt the muscles in my throat seize up. I expected to panic. I *wanted* to panic, the rush of adrenaline. But the evening was too quiet to panic. The air was too soft, too still. If there had been a cold wind, then perhaps I would have panicked. But the most I could manage was to trot from Madison to Fifth Avenue on the way back to my apartment. Then, at the corner of Fifth and Fiftieth Street, in the milky glow of Saint Patrick's, I stopped abruptly. Effect without cause. I hunched forward, my hands on my knees. I breathed in and out. What else could I do?

JANUARY 1, 2001:

For the rest of the year, I did not leave the apartment. I kept to a ten foot radius centered at the phone. (I hadn't bothered to give Holly my mobile number, which I used only for work appointments.) I ate whatever was in the kitchen, frozen pot pies and cocktail franks, and then canned corn sandwiches.

Holly, however, did not call, and with every sunrise my thoughts grew ever more desperate, my mood ever more dismal.

New Year's Eve came and went. I sat next to the phone, the window cracked open; I sat within earshot of Times Square. I sat and wept. No, gentlemen, I do not mention this for pity. Not in the least. For I deserve none and will abide none. But the fact that I wept is indicative of how Holly had, how Holly *has,* cut to the very bone of my existence. As I reread the first pages of this journal, which I did last night, I am struck by the verbal distance, the *stasis,* the ignorant coherence of the words with which I set down my love for her. It *was* a coherent love. Until we kissed. Until I held her in my arms, the logic of what I felt was pure. *What* I desired and *why* I desired it were one and the same. *Video, ergo amo.* But no more. What I desire is still Holly Servant. But now *why* I desire her is as much what I am, what I *am become,* as what she is. I am become a man who wakes up wrenching his head from side to side, who hears her name in the sound of his own swallowing, who notices flecks of blood on the rim of his toilet. These manifestations I cannot account for in rational terms.

JANUARY 3:

Thought and action, gentlemen. Thought and action. How rare to reconcile the two! This afternoon, I contrived and connived and otherwise fibbed to every major airline to discover Holly Servant's flight number for tomorrow. That kind of information is not had without a detailed narrative. From airline to airline, my narrative shifted and evolved. Variously, I was her therapist, her astrologer, her brother, and lastly of course her husband . . . I was a romantic husband too, determined to surprise my wife at the airport on our third anniversary. To show her that the spark had not gone out of our marriage. I had lined up a minister, and we would renew our vows then and there, at the airport, before she boarded the plane . . . for the west coast . . . for who knows how long. . . .

I was choking on the words.

As she gave me the flight information, the reservations clerk began to weep.

JANUARY 4:

ow I shall tell you what happened at the airport. While the moment is still fresh in my mind, I shall tell you what happened. Even though the urge is strong to lie down, to sleep (perchance to dream), I shall tell you of the ordeal at LaGuardia Airport a mere ninety minutes ago.

Because I am too exhausted to switch on the television, I still do not know if the record low temperature was broken this afternoon. The record was, or is, two degrees below zero. That much I know because the radio in the taxi was on. As we careened down Grand Central Parkway towards LaGuardia, the temperature just outside the grimy glass window was zero degrees. The Muslim driver whistled and then called back to me, "Very cold. Very very cold."

"Bum-killer cold," I said.

"Going to Florida?"

"What gave me away?"

"You look like—"

"Like a Jew?"

"Well, yes, but I was going to say you look like you need a vacation."

I thought: If ever a man did not deserve Holly Servant, I was that man.

The wind was like a hard shove in the chest as I climbed out of the taxi in front of the Continental Terminal. Her flight was scheduled to depart within the hour, so I headed straight for the gate. No sign of her. But I was still early. I bought a diet soda from a kiosk and settled into a black polyurethane seat. There I sat for half an hour and nursed the drink as the waiting area filled with people. What I was going to say to her, I hadn't a clue. Her name, to get her attention. But beyond that, I had nothing rehearsed. Purposely, I had nothing rehearsed. I meant to *be* there, to think and to react in the present tense. There was also the fact that I still didn't know why she had disappeared, what had gone wrong. Here is what I feared most: That nothing had gone wrong. That she had, at last, come to her senses. That she had thought through the prospect of the two of us, she and I, together, and had shuddered at the absurdity—and then sprinted downstairs at the Hotel Beverly to check out. That, I could not answer. When a person latches onto the truth, and latches onto it with finality, lies become useless. It's like trying to convince a dog to let go of a steak bone for the chance at a rubber chew stick.

Not the metaphor I dreamed of. But so be it.

Fifteen minutes before her flight was scheduled to take off, I caught sight of her. She wore the red parka from Christmas night, unzipped to reveal the pink sweater from the ice rink. Underneath that, I knew she was naked . . . a recapitulation, in a moment, of the three images I held dearest of her. I rushed up to her and caught her by the right shoulder. "Holly!"

"Leave me alone," she said, softly.

"What happened? What's wrong?"

"Nothing happened. Just go away."

"Why didn't you return my calls?"

She looked me in the eyes, about to cry. Then, suddenly, she slapped me across the face. It was a half-hearted slap, weak in the wrist, which I could have caught, but instead I accepted it with my eyes shut. Her hand against my face, even for an instant, was ecstasy.

Then she said: "Finky told me about *Mark Goldblatt*."

I cringed at the name. "I never intended to lie to you."

"But I guess you just couldn't help yourself," she said.

"It's a sickness," I said. "It has nothing to do with what I felt for you, what I feel for you."

She turned away from me but made no effort to leave; then, a second later, she turned back. She whispered, "Who are you?"

"You know my name."

"Do I?"

"If you want the truth, forget about Mark Goldblatt," I replied. "Mark Goldblatt is a fiction. He's a fiction I created before we ever met. But if he's the reason you're here, if he's the reason you came to New York, then I don't regret a thing. Except that I hurt you. *That* I regret. But I don't regret what I feel for you. I don't regret that I love you. It's the truth, Holly. I love you."

"I don't understand," she cried. "Who wrote the article about the Chinese man?"

Before I could answer, a hand latched onto my shoulder and

spun me around. In front of me stood a short fat man. Finky. He was dressed in an beige blazer, the kind of blazer that a used-car salesman would wear in a parody of used-car salesmen. He looked younger than I had imagined him, about my age. That was the impression I got in the instant before he drove his small fat fist into my abdomen. As I sprawled backwards onto a black polyurethane seat, Holly shouted, "No, don't hurt him!"

Those words from her would have been worth much pain, but in fact he hadn't hurt me. Half a year of the Sunrise Workout had hardened my stomach beyond the kind of blow Finky was able to deliver. As I bounced up from the chair, I saw the fear register in his eyes. He backpedaled a couple of steps, his fists still clenched, now in a sort of half-formed boxer's stance. But no anger was in me. None whatsoever. I turned towards Holly, and I started to tell her again that I loved her. But then another hand caught my shoulder, a much larger hand. This one also jerked me around, much more violently than the first, and in the instant before he drove his huge fist into my face, I saw that it was Broad Nose.

Gentlemen, I lay semi-conscious for perhaps five minutes. When my eyes regained their focus, I saw only a blanket of tissues. My nose felt like a lump of clay stuck haphazardly on my face. The tissues fell away as I sat up; they fell onto my lap, clotted with blood. I had been carried to a high-walled anteroom and laid out on a table. Now I was being restrained by three uniformed men whose breast pockets read AIRPORT SECURITY. Indeed, I felt secure. I began to reel and required them to hold me upright. One of them said to another, "Nah, it's not broken."

"What time is it?" I mumbled.

It was too late. She was gone.

JANUARY 5:

Before I left the airport, a nurse shoved a couple of cotton balls up my nose and told me to leave them there overnight. So I spent much of this morning with a tweezers plucking shreds of bloodied cotton from my nose. In fact, the nose isn't broken; the security man was right. There is no discoloration, and the swelling is minimal. As I stood in front of the mirror, a knock came at the door. Detective Lacuna called out my name, and then he knocked again. I walked to the door, then hesitated. I considered not answering. But what was the use? He would only return later. So I opened the door.

He looked at my face and whistled.

"That bad?" I asked.

"Hold still," he said. He reached towards my face, ran his fingertips lightly up and down the bridge of my nose. Then he lifted both of my eyelids. "No break, no blood in the eyes. My guess is you're going to live."

"That's a comfort," I said.

"Got an official complaint to talk about," he stated. "Seems your buddy Finkleman swore out a complaint as soon as his plane touched down in L.A. He says you attacked one of his clients, the exercise girl."

"What if I did?"

"Did you?"

"No," I said.

"That's what I figured."

"I appreciate your faith."

"The girl got him to drop the charges. But the desk sergeant in L.A. rang up the precinct this morning and asked if we'd send somebody to throw a scare into you. I said I'd do it." He began to grin. "Boo."

"Thanks."

"So this clown Finkleman—is he the one who busted you up?"

"No, that was his employee."

"The guy who was hanging around downstairs?"

"That's the one."

"Want to swear out a counter-complaint?"

"No thanks," I sighed. "Let it end here."

JANUARY 11:

Dear Holly,

No, I've no right to write you again. No right to

trouble you with more words. No right to re-inflict
the memory of me on you after what has happened.
But if I am to recede now from your thoughts, please
permit me these last few lines. That much, I vow:
These will be the last lines I ever write to you. For
I am no writer. That is what I have come to know.
Not that I ever believed I was Mark Goldblatt. But
I wanted you to believe it. Why? For your sake. The
truth of who I was and what I was got overwhelmed
by who and what you imagined me to be. God help
me, but I was seduced by the chance to reinvent
myself in your eyes. Who wouldn't be? For in your
eyes, I have discovered the sum of what I might
have been—had I not become me. The ill-defined,
unmistakable image of all I lack: It is there, in your
eyes, Holly. Your eyes, your voice, your every breath
is a summoning. So it seemed the first moment you
appeared on my TV screen. So it seemed the first
time we kissed. So it seemed as we made love. From
the outset, I have longed to dance in that blesséd
glow. To sing for the angelic host. To bare the vast
prose and poetry of what I feel and be ferried by the
act to a Transcendent Stage.

But I could not do it, I could not perform, not as myself.
The truth of who and what I was would have rendered
the act absurd. But as Mark Goldblatt, Holly, I was
reborn. No, I am reborn. For still I am Mark Goldblatt.
Not the one who scribbled out newspaper columns.
But the one who first loved you. The one who in the
sight of God and man declared what was in his heart.
That Mark Goldblatt is me, no one else.

And you loved me, Holly. There, I've said it: You loved
me. Not what I seemed to be, but what I was, what I am.
Perhaps it was fiction which brought you to me, but it
was truth which delivered you into my arms. If at first
you were moved by words that were not mine, in the end

you cried for my words too. The hand that brushed those tears from your eyes was mine. Remember the truth as well as the fiction. I regret neither.

Nor do I apologize, in retrospect, for what I have done. Nor even for who I am. For I am he who loves you. I cannot apologize for that. Nor alter it. Ever.

love, etc.

JANUARY 12:

The moment I mailed the letter, the pall began to lift. The recollection of my brief interlude with Holly Servant began to assume its abiding shape. For the first time, I was able to peer behind the farce of our final moments, to glimpse once again the dreamlike sweetness of Christmas last. It was a revelation, gentlemen, a miracle weighed against the nightmare at LaGuardia. Now again I have reread the opening pages of this journal, have hearkened once more to my own stated intent: "What I propose is to woo her from afar at first, to woo her with the words love has written upon my heart . . . I will woo her on the page, perchance to bed her by my words."

Gentlemen, what were the odds against success? Though I have lost her, there exists a very literal sense in which I have succeeded. The ache in my heart is perhaps inevitable, given what I undertook. What I would undo is the ache in *her* heart. That is true enough. The grief I caused her, that is my lone regret.

What a renaissance is here, gentlemen!

DOPPELGANGED: A LOVE STORY

(Third Verse)

by Mark Goldblatt

Now where was I? Oh, yes, the Renaissance. Italy, if I'm not mistaken. So there was this traveling

merchant—now, stop me if you've heard this—and
his horse breaks down in the middle of nowhere,
so he walks and walks until at last he finds a
farmhouse. The farmer tells him he can spend the
night, and then he'll give him a lift to town the next
morning. But there's just one catch. He'll have to
share a bedroom with the farmer's daughter. So the
merchant eats his supper, and a few hours later he
heads upstairs. . . .

Oh, then you *have* heard it?

That's all right, I've got a million of 'em.
Like that summer in the Great Northwest when
I boarded with the Spud King, who was anxious
to share his theories about the world. He was a
tall gaunt pipe-cleaner of a man, with the deep
set eyes of a serial killer, who would whittle away
on a stick until it was returned to the nihil from
which the world itself was wrought. Then he
would spit. The spit would freeze in split-seconds
as we watched. We would sit on the porch at his
insistence, the sudden gusts of sub-zero winds
like slaps in the face, and we would stare at the
sky. "See that batch of stars out yonder, just above
the white spruce?"

Yes, I told him, I did.

"That's where they said they was from."

"Who?"

"Aliens."

"Aliens?"

"Damn straight."

"You saw them yourself?"

"With these two eyes."

"Did you talk to them?"

"Sure did," he said.

"What did they say?"

"Two words: Elvis lives."

"Elvis lives? That's all?"

"Then they pointed way out yonder over that white spruce and said, 'Home.'"

"What did they look like?" I inquired.

"Skinny little things. Glowed some."

The wind died down.

"It's an anagram, you know," he said.

"What is?" I asked.

"Elvis lives."

"Oh."

"You know what that means, anagram?"

Yes, I told him, I did.

Now the Spud King had two daughters, Portia and Nervosa. The former had been named for the car in which she was conceived and which, ironically, she came later in life to outweigh. The latter had been named for Elvis, the Spud King asserted, as though the derivation were self-evident.

At this, I rolled my eyes.

But he caught me by the woolen sleeve. "They've both got v's, don't they?"

He forgave me my skepticism, regardless, because he anticipated that I would take one of his daughters as my wife. So he would slap Portia on the rump as she waddled through the front yard, and the ponds of flesh below her cutoff jeans would ripple in concentric waves. "Good loins," he would declare. "Birthin' loins." He was on the whole less optimistic when it came to Nervosa. He would grab her around the waist with his thumb and forefinger and draw attention to the fullness of her lips. "Half her body weight is pink," he'd swear. "Suck a golf ball right through a garden hose. Do you know what I'm saying, boy? Am I getting across to you?"

"Yes, I think so," I replied.

"Go on, baby girl. Give the boy a blow job."

But I pushed her away. "That won't be necessary."

"Just trying to make a point, boy. No offense meant."

"None taken," I assured him.

Portia and Nervosa were in fact a perfect ten—provided that Portia stood on the right. But I was never one for the hard sell, so I begged off. Even after Nervosa showed up one evening at my bedside wearing only a pair of doughnuts, I would not bite. She wriggled free and begged me to lick the powder from her hips. But I've always been a cannoli man myself. Sugary as a southern girl's yes. So I sent Nervosa on her way. She cried, threatened to kill herself. She yanked out a loose thread from the bed sheet and tied a noose in it. But I called her bluff. Then she threatened to turn sideways and disappear.

I only folded my arms.

Portia made her play the next night. The Spud King had sent me out to the barn on an obscure pretext, *Semiotics 101* if memory serves, which made me suspicious because the barn was where Portia slept. I entered soundlessly; the doors were still slick from the grease we used to slide her in and out. Portia sat against the far wall. She wore a sheer negligee—actually seven or eight of them sewn together. The barn was limned by a single lantern, set off to the side, so as to diminish the effect of her enormity. She glanced down as I strolled in. Before her were placed three caskets. She gazed at these significantly.

"What's in the caskets?" I asked.

"Snacks," she replied. "That's all."

"Am I supposed to choose one?"

"Only if you bring me another."

So I sat down across from her.

"You know," she said, "beauty is in the eye of the beholder. Certain societies in the past would have considered a woman like me a sex object."

"Maybe the ones that worshipped asteroids," I offered.

She began to weep at the remark. She covered her face with her hands and cried into them. The liquid flesh of her shoulders and upper arms registered each sob, and I felt bad; I had not intended to hurt her feelings. I had only meant to work up to a banter, to smooth out an awkward moment.

After the sobs subsided, she looked up at me with an ironic smile. The tears still glistened, but the irony of her smile was filled with comprehension and resignation. It was a heartbreaking expression. She said in a soft voice, "It's not your fault. I know I'm overweight."

"That's not true," I objected. "You're just big-boned."

"Big bones," she said, "wrapped in mountains of fat."

"I wouldn't say mountains—"

"It's not your fault," she repeated, this time with an airy laugh. "You're just an Izzy. Daddy explained about men to me when I was just a girl. He told me about the two kinds of men in the world."

"Just two?"

"Iffy and Izzy."

"But my name is—"

"Izzy looks at the world the way it is," she continued. "He sees a piece of clay, and all he sees is a piece of clay. He has no insight, no vision. He judges a thing by its surface, by what is. Get it? Daddy told me that I was never going to marry Izzy."

"What about Iffy?"

"Iffy looks at the world the way it might be,"
she said. "He sees things kind of inside-out. That's
what Daddy likes to call insight. Iffy sees the same
clay as Izzy, but he sees what the clay might become.
What the clay might be *if.* Iffy sees the if in things.
That's what Izzy misses. Daddy said that sooner or
later Iffy was going to come along and marry me."

So I kissed her on the forehead. It was a light
kiss that skimmed the film of perspiration across her
brow. She did not react to the gesture, did not raise
the hulking mass of her arms. She only sat with her
back congealing against the wall and allowed me to
kiss her forehead. She tasted of gravity.

"Besides," she added, "Daddy told me that Izzy
was nothing but a dirty Christ-killer who got what
he deserved in World War Two."

"Out of the mouths of babes," shouted Guy
Gunther, eavesdropping from the hay loft.

Then he leaped down and started towards the
scythe.

JANUARY 14:

Zezel was apologizing for the chloroform even as its effects
began to wear off. The sound of his voice was distant at first,
scratchy, as the fog inside my brain dissolved, and as I realized
that he'd handcuffed my wrists to the steel frame of the bed. I gave the
handcuffs a few perfunctory tugs and then settled back again onto the
mattress.

". . . I consulted several distinguished professors, including a
pharmacologist," he was saying, "and was assured that you would
experience no lingering side effects, no headaches, no nausea."
"I'm all right," I said.
He smiled at the sound of my voice. "No priapism, I trust."
I rattled the handcuffs again. "That a man's reach should exceed
his grasp."
Zezel walked over to the bed, still smiling. "I've written another

story, a sequel of sorts. Perhaps I'll make a book of it yet. It's on your hard drive."

"I look forward to reading it."

"I think it's the finest prose I've written in ages."

There was a pause of several seconds.

"Well?" he said, finally.

"Well, what?"

"Aren't you going to inquire?"

"Why did you chloroform me and handcuff me to the bed?"

"No, not that!"

"But it is a matter of keen interest to me," I said.

"Aren't you going to inquire about Guy Gunther?"

"The character from your story?"

"You *did* read it, didn't you?" he asked ominously.

"In one sitting," I said. "What about Guy Gunther?"

"The truest creation I ever put to paper," he stated.

"What about him?"

"He is the *raison d'être* of the entire cycle."

"Which is significant because?"

"He is you. You are he. You are Guy Gunther."

"*I'm* Guy Gunther?" I said.

"And I, as always, the nameless narrator."

I thought for a moment: "Then why am I the one handcuffed to the bed?"

Zezel seemed startled by the question; he began to scratch his chin. "It *is* rather a paradox. That much, I'll admit. Still, you did kill Aubrey Collins—"

"What?"

"You are the villain, are you not?"

"No!"

"Then who?"

"It was a homeless guy. He confessed before Christmas."

"Why?"

"Why did he confess? Or why did he kill Aubrey Collins?"

"The latter," Zezel said.

"He was a crackhead. He killed Aubrey Collins for cash."

"Are you certain?"

"Lacuna is certain," I said. "That's good enough for me."

He began to scratch his chin again, and then he sighed.

"Sorry," I managed.

"It *is* rather a let down. I had such high hopes for you."

"Maybe next time."

He shook his head gloomily. "No, I fear that your moment in the sun has passed, that it has gone once more into eclipse. The *diem* was there to be *carpéd*. The tide was at the menstrual flood."

I grinned at him. "Still, it wasn't *my* finger in the dike."

"Low shtick! Low shtick!"

"Life is limbo," I said. "Limbo is life."

"Bold talk for a unarmed bandit."

"How so?" I asked.

"J'accuse!" He pointed at me.

"Again, how so?"

"You have stolen my dreams."

"You never had a dream in your life!"

"True, but if I had, you'd have stolen it."

"You handcuffed me on a hypothetical?"

"The manacles, at least, are not mind-forged."

I gave the handcuffs another tug. "No."

"Now," he continued, "on to the Inquisition."

"I confess."

"Not so fast—"

"I retract."

"I knew it!" He sat down beside me on the bed. "About my wife . . . what say you, Infidel?"

"With respect to?"

"She's a bit of a squeeze, isn't she? Tight as a snare drum, and she doesn't get very wet. Plus, she gives head like a bellows. No imagination whatsoever, am I right?"

"I don't remember."

He wheeled suddenly and slapped me across the face. Then, an instant later, he was smiling again. "Regardless, that's a personal matter. Between you and my wife. None of my affair. I withdraw the question. Do you forgive me?"

"The man in handcuffs always forgives," I said.

His expression altered. "I've broken off with Allison Molho."

"I'm sorry."

"*Felix culpa*," he replied. "The cat is to blame."

"The man in handcuffs always apologizes."

He nodded. "The man in handcuffs has many burdens."

"Why did you break off with her?"

"I could never be the apple of her eye."

"Nor the leaven in her loaf," I said.

"Nor even the snake in her garden."

"Please," I said, "take off the handcuffs."

"Not quite yet."

"Why not?"

"I want to perform an experiment." He turned and dashed into the kitchen. There followed the sound of a drawer sliding open and shut, then footsteps back and forth, then the sound of the draw sliding open and shut again. When Zezel reappeared at the threshold of the kitchen, he was holding a butcher knife in his hand. My heart started to pound at the sight of it. He returned at a trot to the bedside. He stood over me; I lay still and smiled at him. He leaned forward, steadied himself with a knee on the edge of the mattress, and flashed the knife in the direction of my face. I did not flinch; the effort not to flinch caused the muscles in my throat to quiver. Then he waved the knife within half an inch of my nose. It smelled slightly of meat. Then he touched the blunt edge to my cheek, the cheek he had slapped a minute before, then traced the contours of my chin and mouth with the tip. The blade was cool against my skin. He looked straight into my eyes. He seemed to will me to close them—which I was reluctant to do. But after several second I did, reflexively. As soon as I closed my eyes, he spoke to me again. "Do you think I'm insane?"

"No," I responded, weakly.

He poked me in the cheek with the tip of the blade. "Don't patronize me."

"All right, I'm not certain."

"There is much to argue that I *am* insane," Zezel said, without emotion. "Not the least of which is the fact that I've manacled my best friend to his own bed and waved a butcher knife in front of his face."

"Weighty evidence."

"Indeed and indeed."

"But not conclusive."

"No, not conclusive," he said. "What if, however, I were to pass the blade across your breast? Not very deep, not deep enough to draw blood. But deep enough to mark the flesh. What would you conclude in that case?" He drew the cutting edge of the knife across my chest, nipple to nipple, careful not to break the skin. As I began to shake, he stopped. "Without a doubt, to cut out your heart would mark me insane. Or at minimum exceptionally Semitic. Not to mention the disappointment it would cause you. Still, what intrigues me is the exact point at which insanity becomes certain. If a man has seven layers of skin, how many of these might another man lay open and still lay claim to some measure of sanity?"

"Hypothetically?"

"Of course."

"Then I'd have to answer six," I replied. "Blood is the logical litmus in the case you describe."

He withdrew the knife and stepped back. "Then I am not insane. For I would not forfeit our friendship. No, not even for a pound of flesh."

"What about the handcuffs?"

He grinned. "I am content."

He went into his pants pocket and came out with a ring of two metal keys. He undid the right handcuff; the left he left to me. As I struggled with the lock, he walked back into the kitchen. I heard the drawer slide open again, heard him replace the knife. Then I heard the drawer slide shut. He returned to the bedside just as I freed myself. He sat down next to me and reached for my right hand. His voice was low and full of concern. "Did the steel burn your wrist?"

"Not too much," I said.

"There's ointment, I believe, in the bathroom."

"Maybe later."

"No ointment for your heart though," he said.

So we sat, the two of us, shoulder to shoulder, on the edge of the bed. Neither of us spoke now; the air was warm and heavy with our silence. Then, after a minute, simultaneously, we sighed.

I glanced down at the handcuffs, which were lying on the floor at the foot of the bed; then, at last, I turned to him. "Why?"

"I suspected you of cold-blooded murder."

"Ah."

"Anyway," he added, "you can't be too careful."

"These kids today with their crazy dances. . . ."

He turned to face me. "So there's no chance?"

"That I'm a cold-blooded murderer? No."

"Still, you *have* been under stress. Perhaps you blacked out and committed the crime. There are precedents in the *film noir*—"

"No," I said, with more force.

He clasped my right hand. "As for the exercise girl, despair not."

I closed my eyes.

"Plenty of fish in the ocean." He winked at me. "And vice-versa."

"Or I could cut bait."

"I would be your Heloise," he said. "Your Lorena if you faltered."

"John Wayne never falters. He just climbs back on the whores."

Zezel kissed me wetly on the cheek. "You are the love of my life."

"I know," I said.

"Still, I must *fuck* someone."

"Clearly."

"*Ergo*, I am going to reconcile with my wedded wife."

"Just like that?" I asked. "You'll rekindle her heart?"

"On the contrary, she will require a blood sacrifice."

"How so?"

He grinned coyly at me. "Just remember that I love you."

I squinted at him and tried to read his eyes.

Zezel reared back suddenly and punched me in the nose. The blow knocked me off the bed and onto the floor, and I began rolling back and forth in pain, covering my face with my hands. I realized at once he had broken my nose; I heard the weakened cartilage crackle beneath his fist, and simultaneously I tasted blood in the back of my throat. Then, a moment later, I felt a hand, a gentle hand, on my shoulder. Between my fingers, I glimpsed Zezel kneeling over me. He was whispering, "There was no other way—"

The words filled me with rage. I lashed out with my right leg, caught him with the instep of my right foot against his left cheek. The force of the kick sent him sprawling backwards, and I heard the clang of his head against the metal frame of the bed. From that clang, I knew he was significantly injured. I looked up as he slumped forward in a heap.

Warily, I crawled over to him. My left hand was still cupping my nose; blood was dripping through my fingers onto the wood floor. Then I muttered his name. I muttered his name three times. He did not move.

I laid hold of his scant blond hair with my bloody left hand and lifted up his head. His face was ashen, his eyes open but glassy. As I drew back my hand, it was soaked and sticky with blood—Zezel's and mine. Our two bloods, Zezel's and mine, were mingling in the palm of my left hand.

"But why?" I asked him.

"My wife . . . call her."

"I'm calling an ambulance."

"Yes, but then her," he said.

"Why?"

"So she'll see us as we are."

"And?"

"I'll tell her we fought for her honor."

I slumped down next to him and began to laugh. Our backs were up against the side of the bed; again, we sat shoulder to shoulder. He reached down and held my free hand.

I said, "She'll never let you play with me again."

"No," he coughed, "but that's the beauty of it."

"How so?"

He rested his head on my shoulder. "Now, I'll have to cheat on her with *you*."

The two of us laughed softly, and he squeezed my hand. For several moments, we sat there, on the floor, beside the bed, and continued to laugh. Then, as I felt him drifting out of consciousness, I rose up and dialed nine-one-one.

∽

I left Zezel at the emergency room of the hospital in the arms of his wife. He had, as it turned out, suffered a mild concussion, and the cut in the back of his skull took seventeen stitches to close. These details I learned just moments ago from Mrs. Zezel—who phoned from the hospital. "So he picked me, kiddo," she added. "Sorry, but that's the way the cookie crumbles. He said he broke your nose. Sorry about that too. But you had an ass-kicking coming. Even you've got to admit it."

"I do," I said.

JANUARY 16:

The snow that fell overnight dusted the morning sidewalks, a dull white patina of ice that crunched underfoot as I walked down Sixth Avenue to the University, to Room 21B4. The wind blew in my face; it chilled the salve beneath the bandages that covered my nose. I leaned into it, the wind. It had a numbing effect.

Penelope Estes frowned at me as I stepped into the office. "You missed the last prick."

"I know. I apologize."

"Was there a reason?"

"It's personal," I said.

She sighed, leaned back in her chair. "Did you run out of pills?"

"Only this morning."

"What happened to your nose?"

I smiled. "It's personal."

"It's broken, isn't it?"

"Yes."

"You've got raccoon eyes. That's how you can tell when it's broken."

"It also makes a bad noise inside your head," I said.

"So you don't want to tell me how you broke your nose?"

I thought for a moment. "I stared too hard into the abyss."

She shook her head, then leaned forward again. "Ready?"

"Yes."

She lifted her clipboard to check off my answers. "Effects?"

"None that I know of," I said.

"Depression?"

"No."

"Euphoria?"

"No."

"Paranoia?"

"No more than usual."

She set down the clipboard. "Well, then, I guess that's it."

I put out my hand for the next month's supply of green pills.

Now, at last, she began to smile. "No, I mean, *that's it*."

"That's it?"

"Your six month interval is over. It's the end of the study."

Finally, I grasped the situation. "I'm of no more use to you?"

"That's a not a very kind choice of words. I'd prefer to think that you've fulfilled your obligation." She reached into the desk drawer and handed me a last hundred dollar bill. "On behalf of the entire project, I'd like to express our gratitude—"

"So what was I?"

"In what sense?"

"Control group or test group?"

She shook her head again. "Sorry, I can't give out that information."

"Not even for a cool hundred dollars?" I offered the bill back across the desk.

She exhaled and smiled at the gesture. "Not even for a cool hundred dollars."

JANUARY 21:

ezel left a note taped to the door, the first I've heard from him since I left him at the hospital. The note was a poem titled "Life":

LIFE

by Mark Goldblatt

We do what we must.
We do what we can.
We do what we don't.
It's part of the plan.

> We don't what we might.
> We might but we won't.
> We should come tomorrow.
> But somehow we don't.

Gentlemen, I have read the poem at least a dozen times. I cannot make the slightest sense of it. But I like how it sounds. What more is required of a poem? On that note, therefore, I end this journal.

JUNE 8:

Holly Servant has returned to my arms! She called last night from the Continental Terminal at LaGuardia and asked if I wanted to meet her at the airport for a cup of coffee. When I arrived, she had seven suitcases at her feet. I did not kiss her; I dared not. I took her hand in mine, pressed it, then let go a second later.

"Where's the coffee shop?" I said softly.

"Please, can we go somewhere else?"

The two of us managed her luggage to the terminal exit and then, with the aid of a skycap, into the trunk of a waiting cab. As we climbed into the back seat, I asked her where she wanted to go. Suddenly, she began to weep. She grabbed my right hand and brought it to her mouth; she kissed it lightly. Then, still clutching my hand, she closed her eyes.

The driver, a young Israeli with a shaven head, knocked twice on the plexiglass divider for directions. I shrugged, glanced back at Holly, then shrugged again. Finally, I inhaled and gave him directions to my apartment.

Gentlemen: I'll not belabor what occurred between us. Suffice it to say that Holly has relocated to Manhattan, has signed a contract through her new agent to represent a line of sportswear for women. No more stunt work. She is scheduled, the day after tomorrow, to read for a minor role on *One Life to Live*. After we arrived at my apartment, Holly kissed me on the lips. Then I ran downstairs to the corner market for coffee—which she brewed in the pot under the stove.

No, gentlemen, we did not make love last night. But we slept side by side, and when I awakened I found her still asleep next to me. I kissed her lightly on the shoulder, and she opened her eyes. Only for a moment, only long enough to smile. Then she fell back asleep.

After breakfast, Holly unpacked two of her bags. The last five she didn't unpack. She is going to look for her own studio apartment next week, after the soap opera audition. That is her plan. Even as I write, however, I can hear her humming in the kitchen. I don't doubt she is chopping and dicing and tearing the vegetables we bought this afternoon into a high protein, low cholesterol dinner salad. Now, as the evening mists arise from the city below us, and as narrow diminutions of light seep through the venetian blinds, I see no shadow of another parting from her.

ABOUT THE AUTHOR:

Mark Goldblatt is a political columnist, novelist, essayist and book reviewer who teaches at Fashion Institute of Technology of the State University of New York. His work has appeared in *The New York Post*, *The New York Times*, *USA Today*, *The Daily News*, *Newsday*, *National Review*, *The New English Review*, *The American Spectator*, *The Common Review*, *Commentary*, *Reason*, *Philosophy Now* and the webzine *Ducts*. His first novel, *Africa Speaks*, was published by Permanent Press in 2002.

To read more, visit *www.markgoldblatt.com*.

www.ingramcontent.com/pod-product-compliance
Lightning Source LLC
Chambersburg PA
CBHW020651260626
47157CB00008B/2995